To Wilson, Elena and Liliana.

To my friends, who are also my teachers.

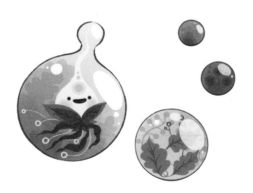

· Lorena Alvarez ·

Hicotea

A Nightlights Story

Nobrow
London | New York

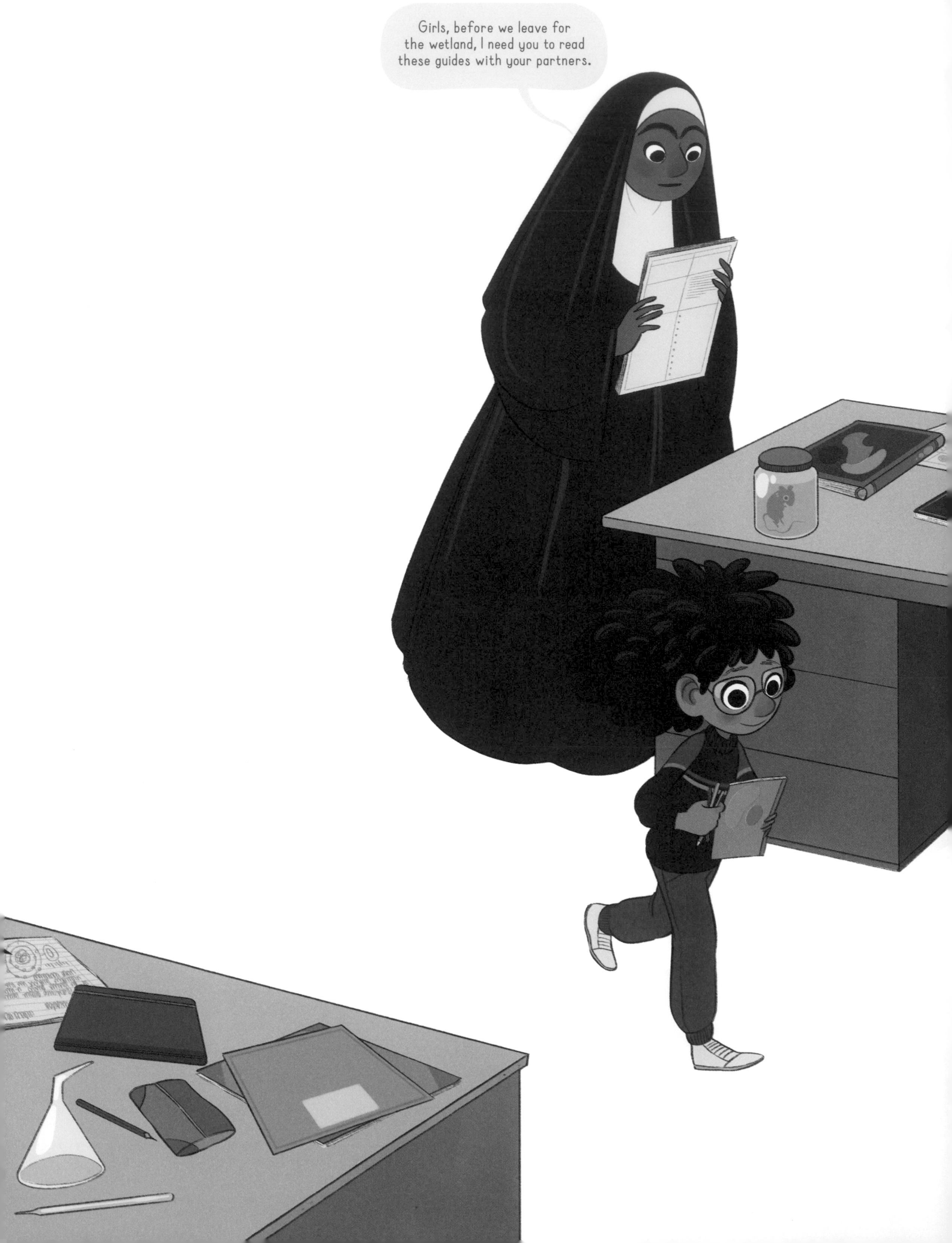
Girls, before we leave for the wetland, I need you to read these guides with your partners.

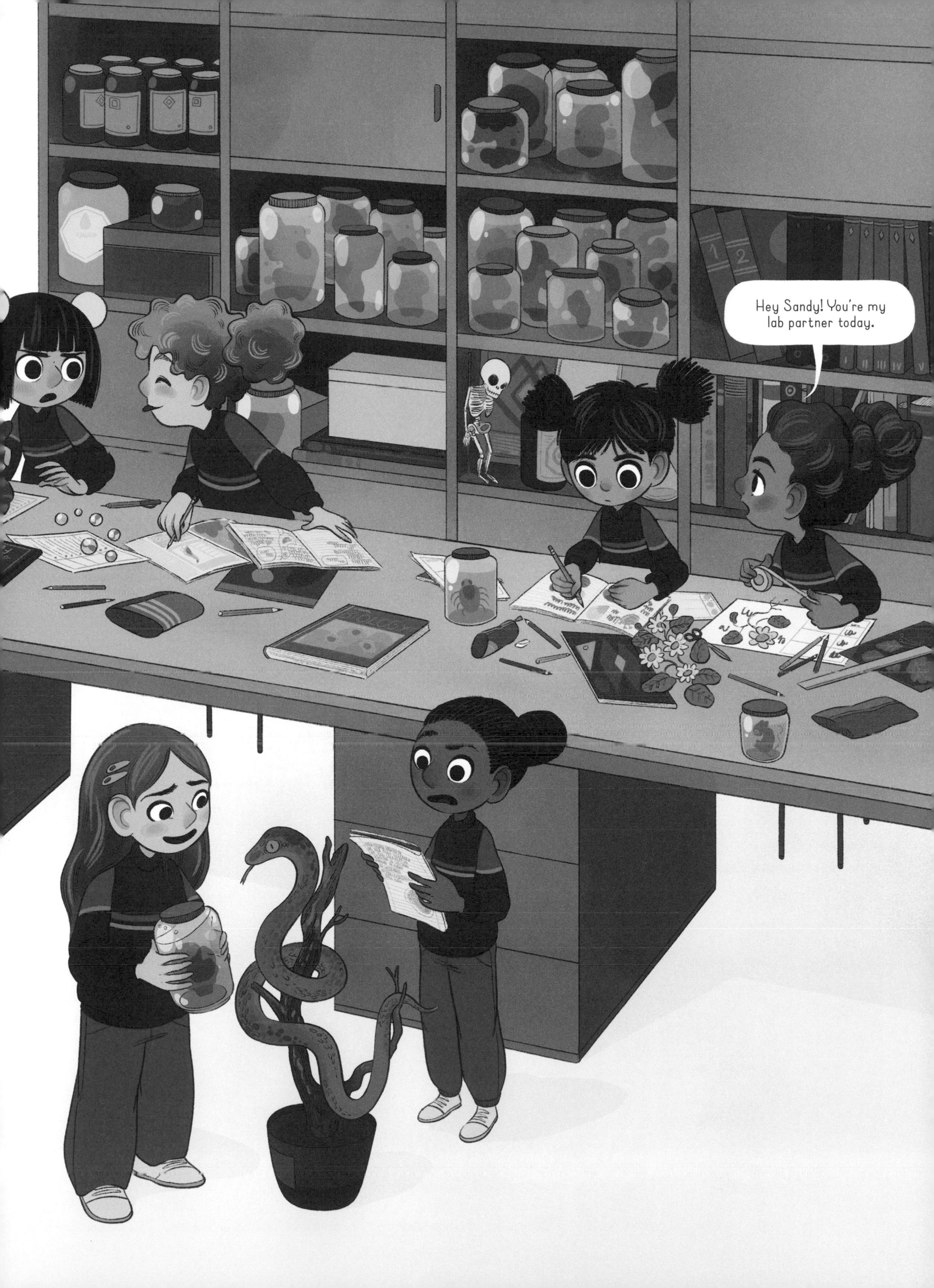
Hey Sandy! You're my lab partner today.

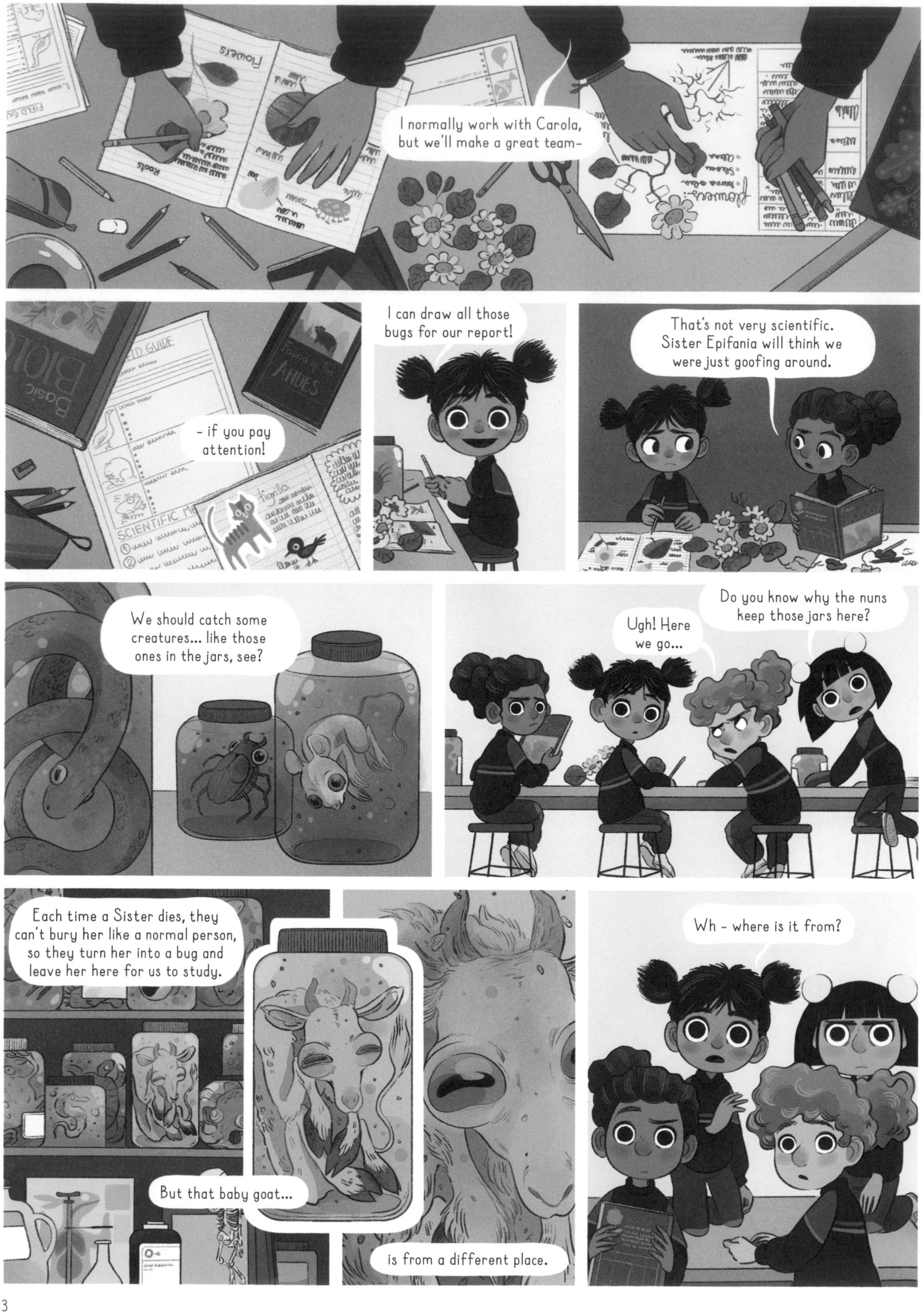
I normally work with Carola, but we'll make a great team-
- if you pay attention!
I can draw all those bugs for our report!
That's not very scientific. Sister Epifania will think we were just goofing around.
We should catch some creatures... like those ones in the jars, see?
Ugh! Here we go...
Do you know why the nuns keep those jars here?
Each time a Sister dies, they can't bury her like a normal person, so they turn her into a bug and leave her here for us to study.
But that baby goat...
is from a different place.
Wh - where is it from?

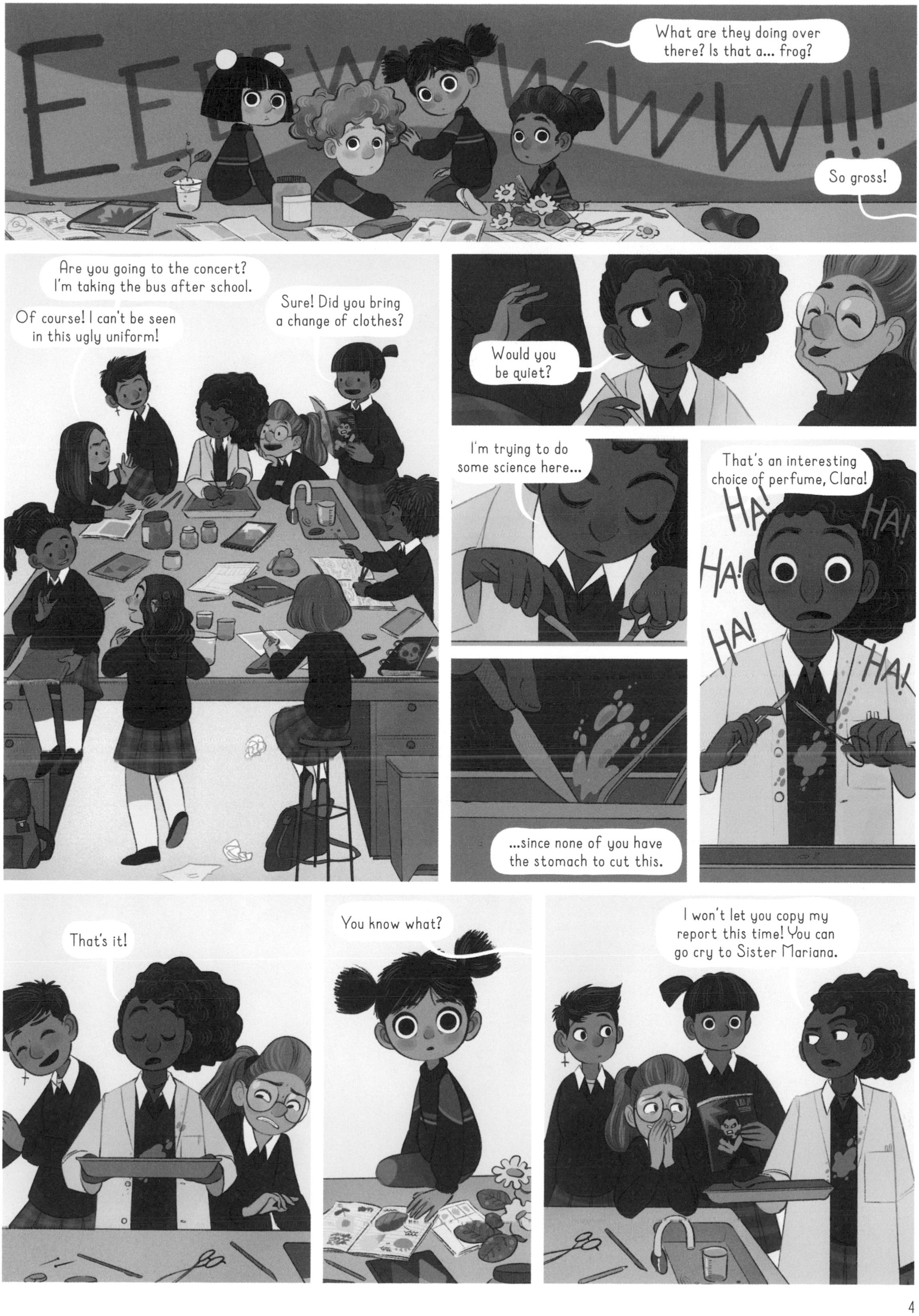
EEEWWWWWW!!!
What are they doing over there? Is that a... frog?
So gross!
Are you going to the concert? I'm taking the bus after school.
Of course! I can't be seen in this ugly uniform!
Sure! Did you bring a change of clothes?
Would you be quiet?
I'm trying to do some science here...
...since none of you have the stomach to cut this.
That's an interesting choice of perfume, Clara!
HA! HA! HA! HA! HA!
That's it!
You know what?
I won't let you copy my report this time! You can go cry to Sister Mariana.

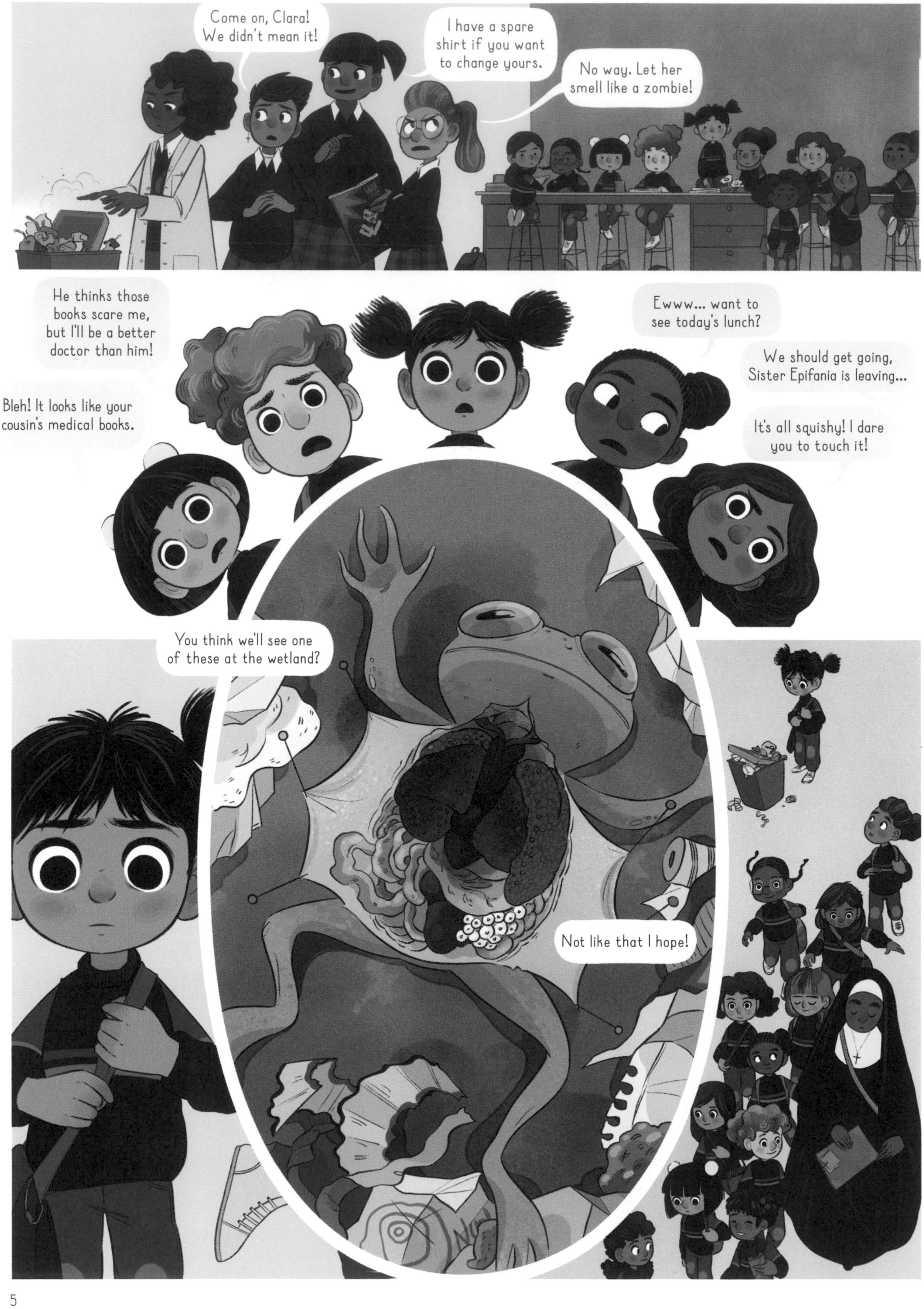
Come on, Clara! We didn't mean it!
I have a spare shirt if you want to change yours.
No way. Let her smell like a zombie!
He thinks those books scare me, but I'll be a better doctor than him!
Bleh! It looks like your cousin's medical books.
Ewww... want to see today's lunch?
We should get going, Sister Epifania is leaving...
It's all squishy! I dare you to touch it!
You think we'll see one of these at the wetland?
Not like that I hope!

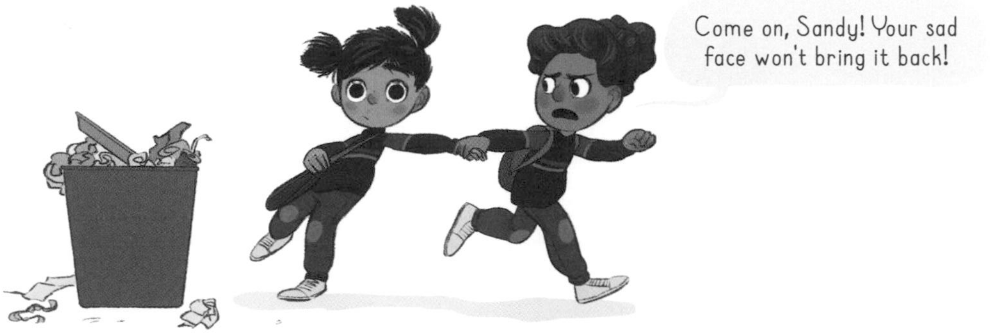
Come on, Sandy! Your sad face won't bring it back!

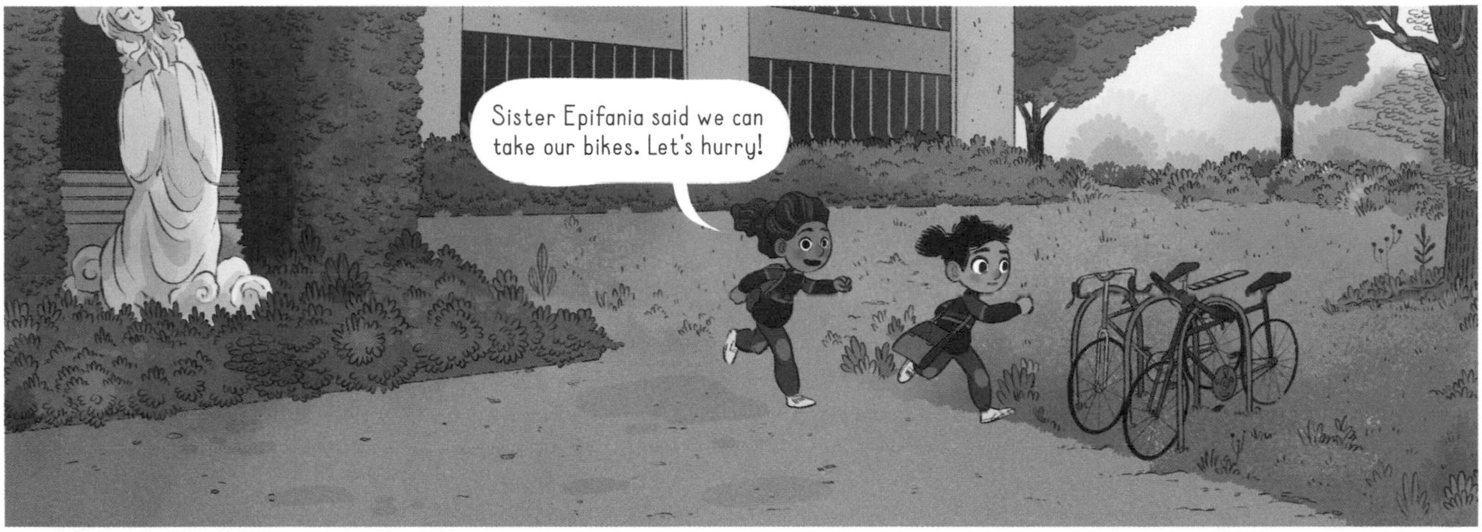
Sister Epifania said we can take our bikes. Let's hurry!

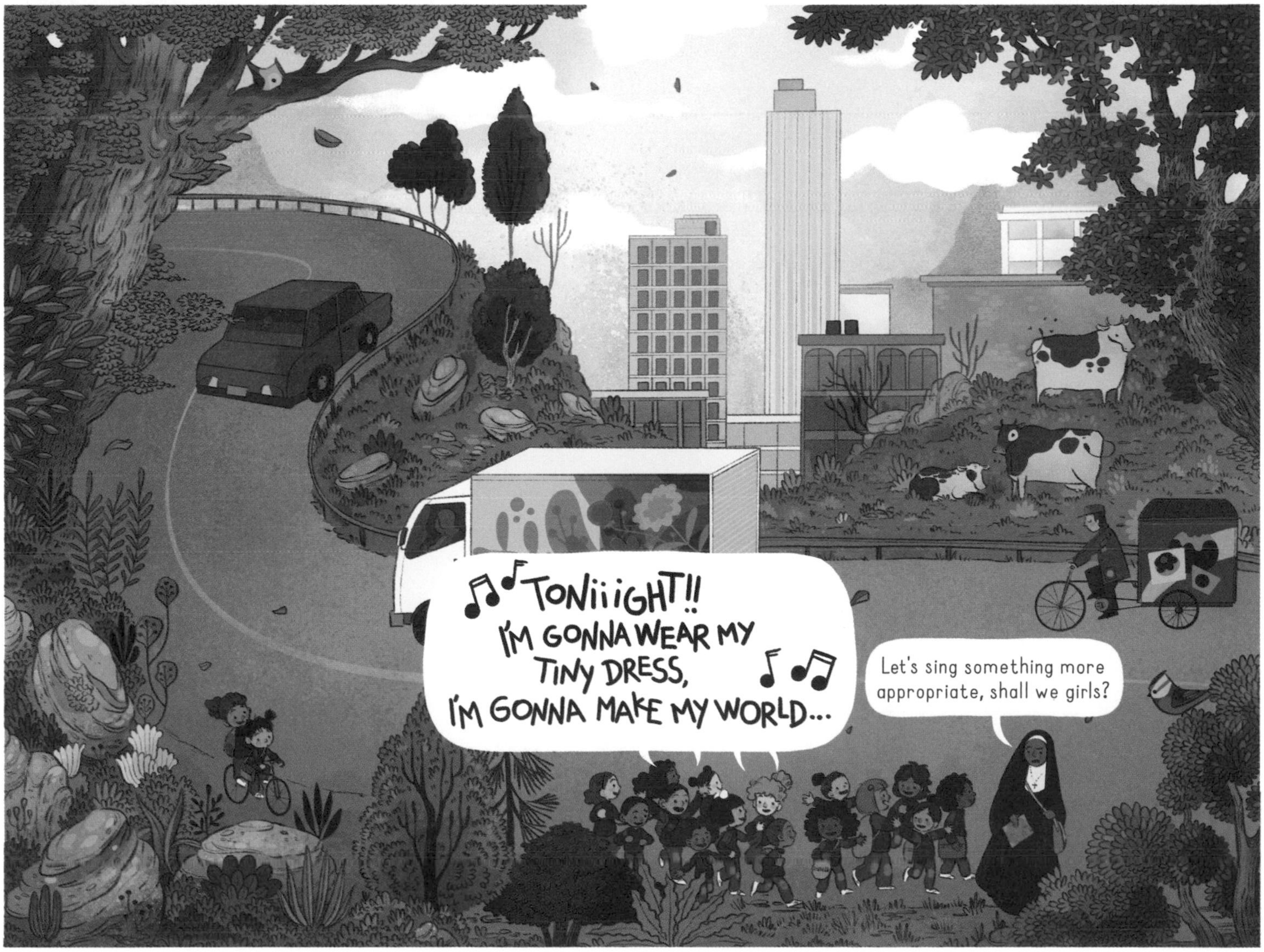
TONiiiGHT!! I'M GONNA WEAR MY TINY DRESS, I'M GONNA MAKE MY WORLD...
Let's sing something more appropriate, shall we girls?

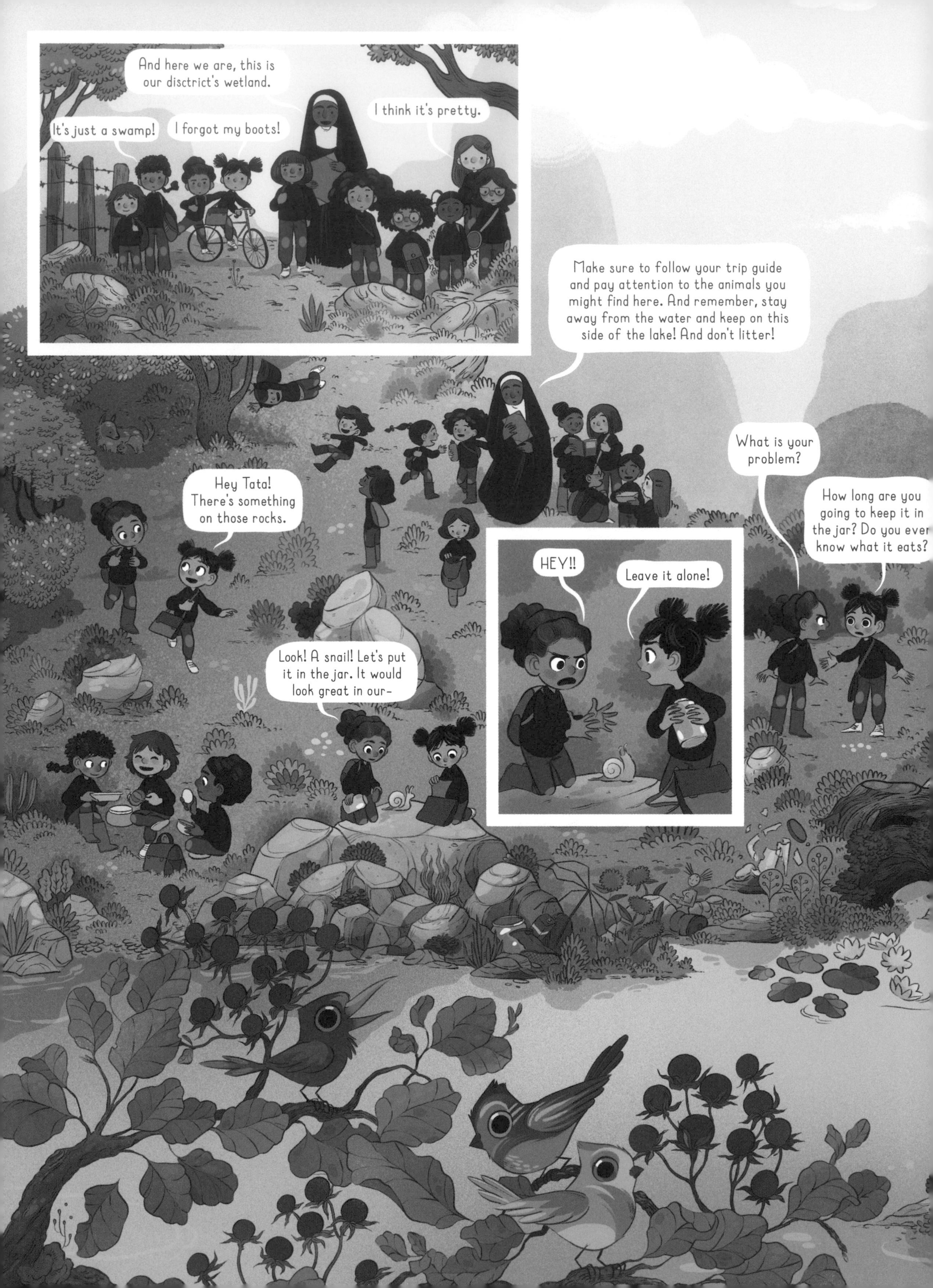
And here we are, this is our disctrict's wetland.
It's just a swamp!
I forgot my boots!
I think it's pretty.
Make sure to follow your trip guide and pay attention to the animals you might find here. And remember, stay away from the water and keep on this side of the lake! And don't litter!
Hey Tata! There's something on those rocks.
Look! A snail! Let's put it in the jar. It would look great in our-
HEY!!
Leave it alone!
What is your problem?
How long are you going to keep it in the jar? Do you ever know what it eats?

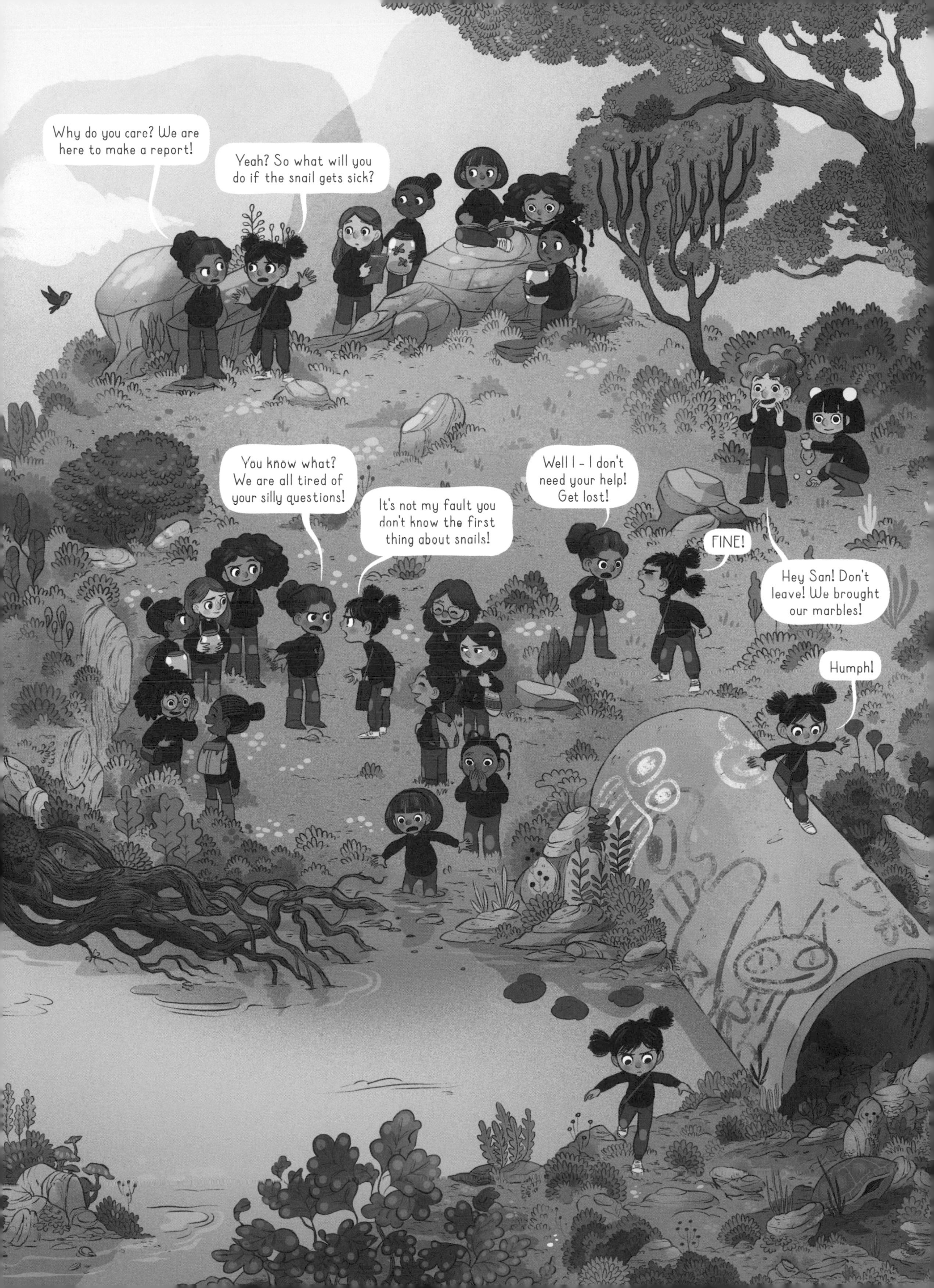
Why do you care? We are here to make a report!
Yeah? So what will you do if the snail gets sick?
You know what? We are all tired of your silly questions!
It's not my fault you don't know the first thing about snails!
Well I - I don't need your help! Get lost!
FINE!
Hey San! Don't leave! We brought our marbles!
Humph!

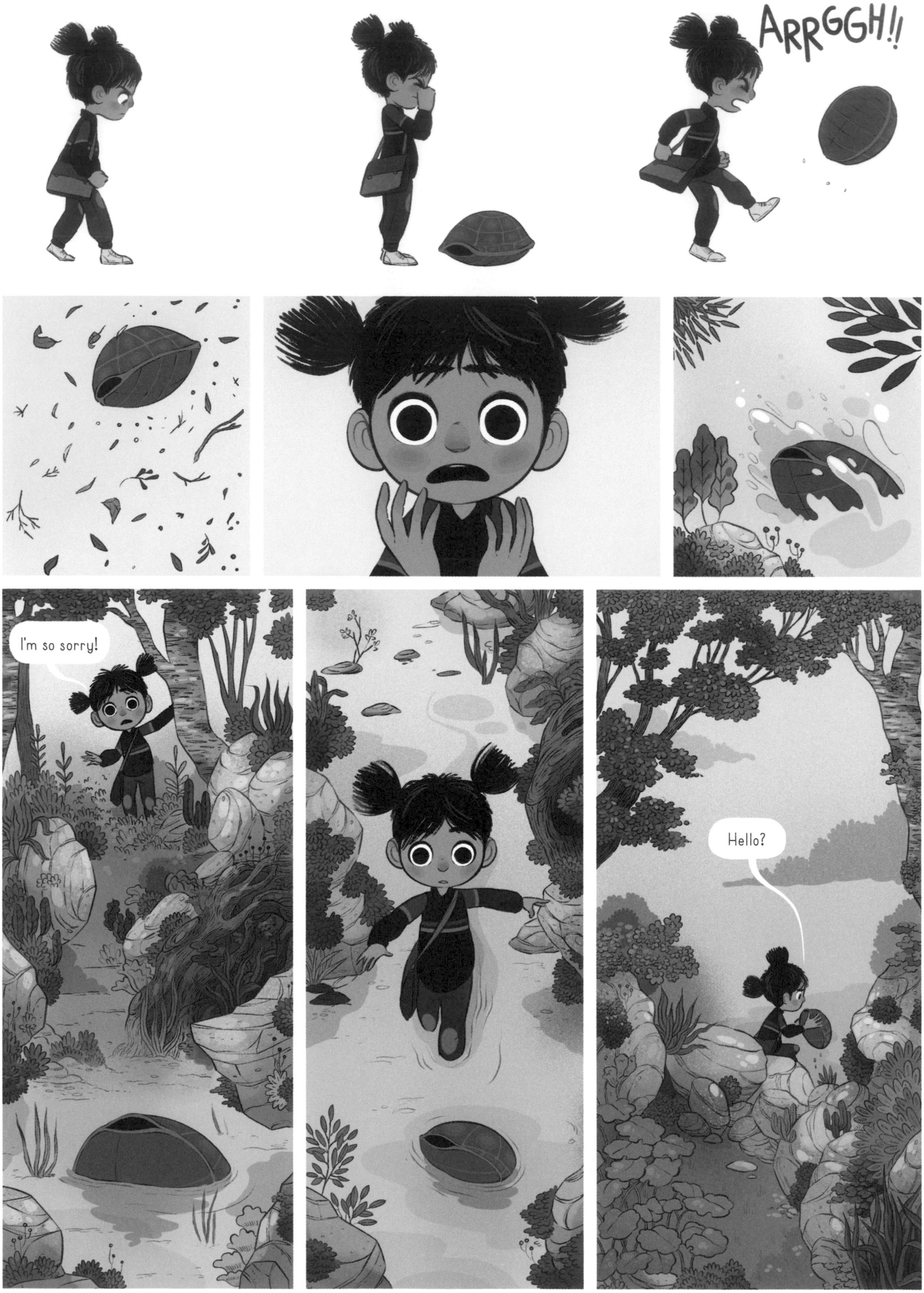
ARRGGH!!
I'm so sorry!
Hello?

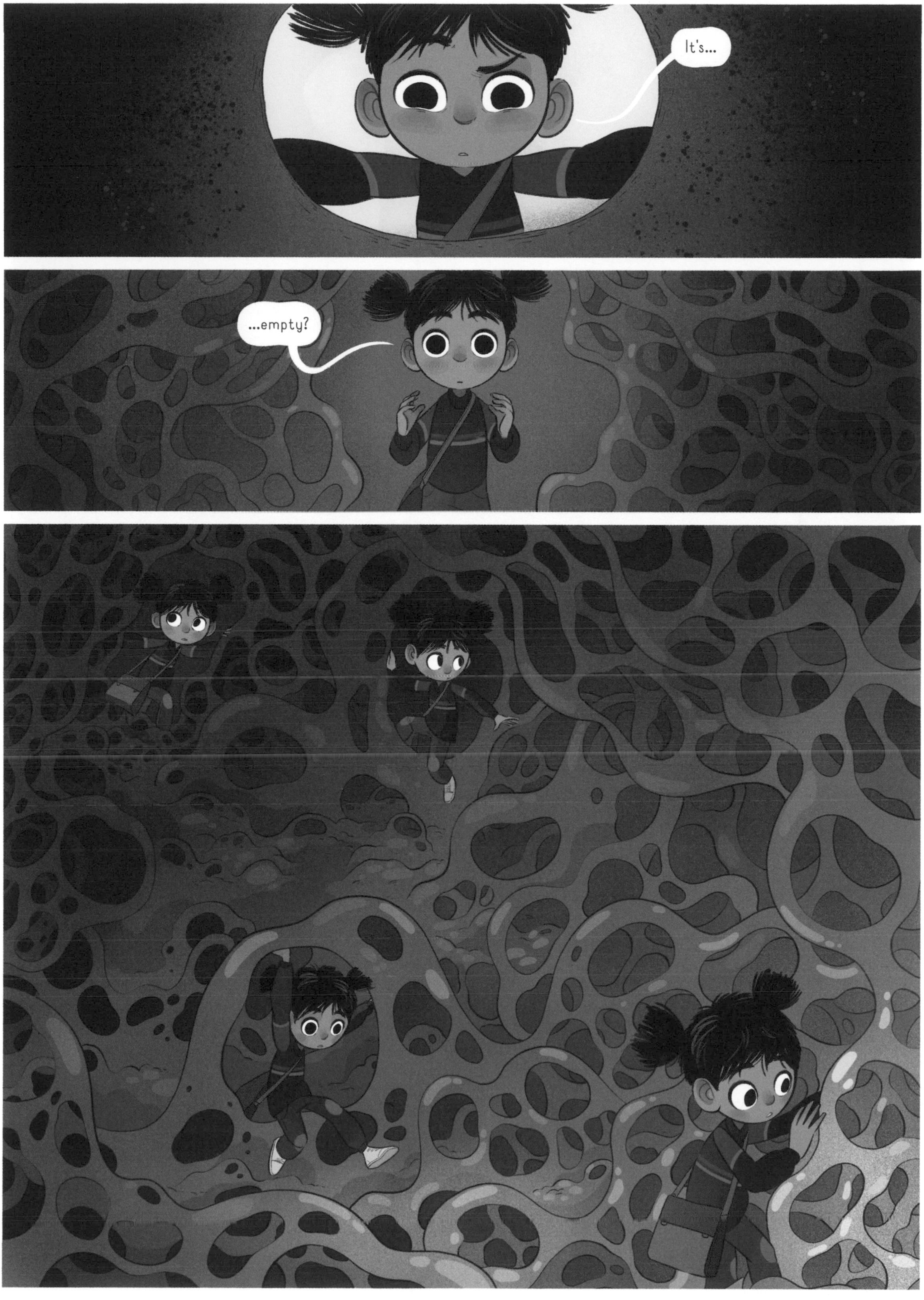
It's...
...empty?

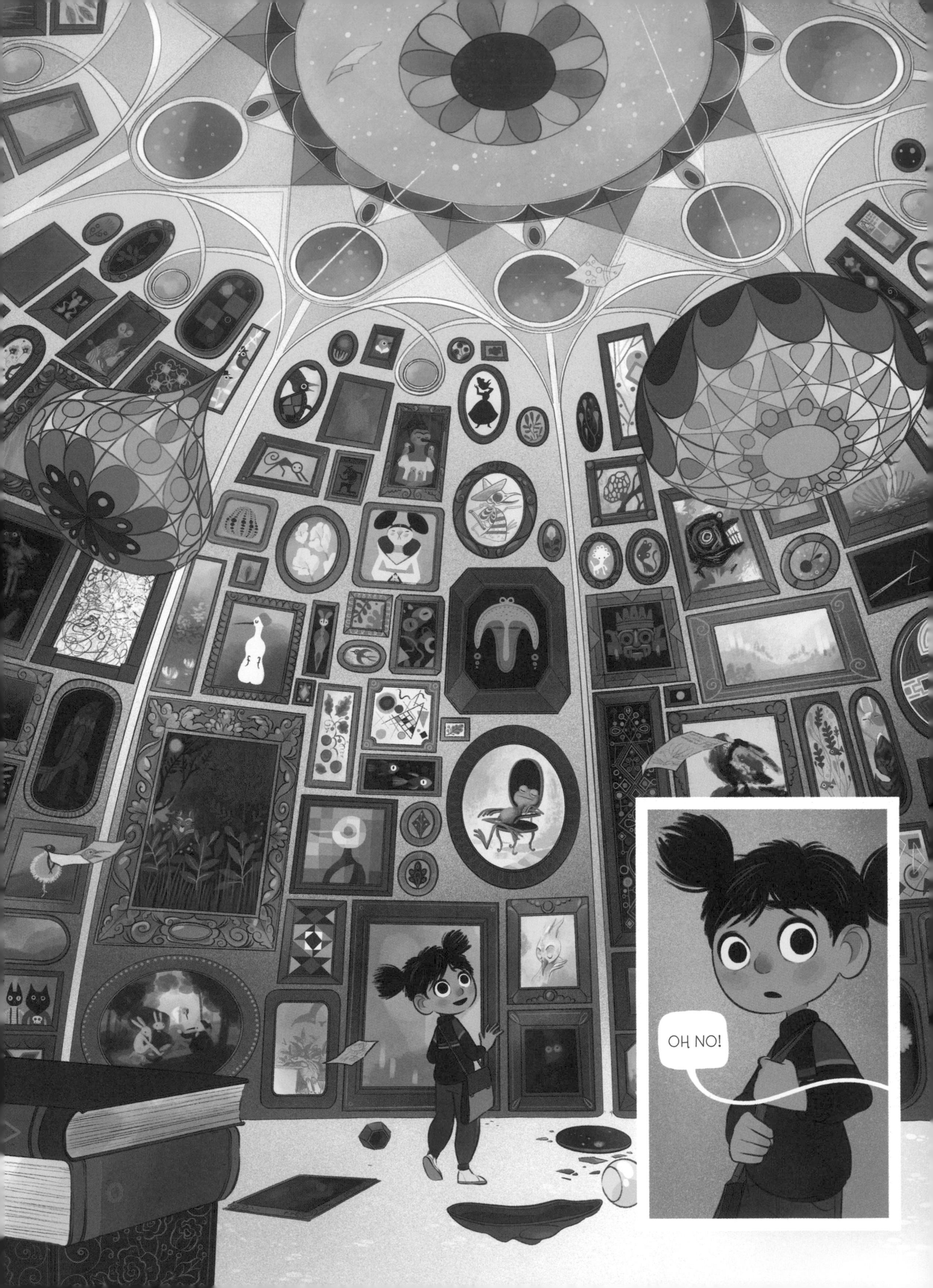
OH NO!

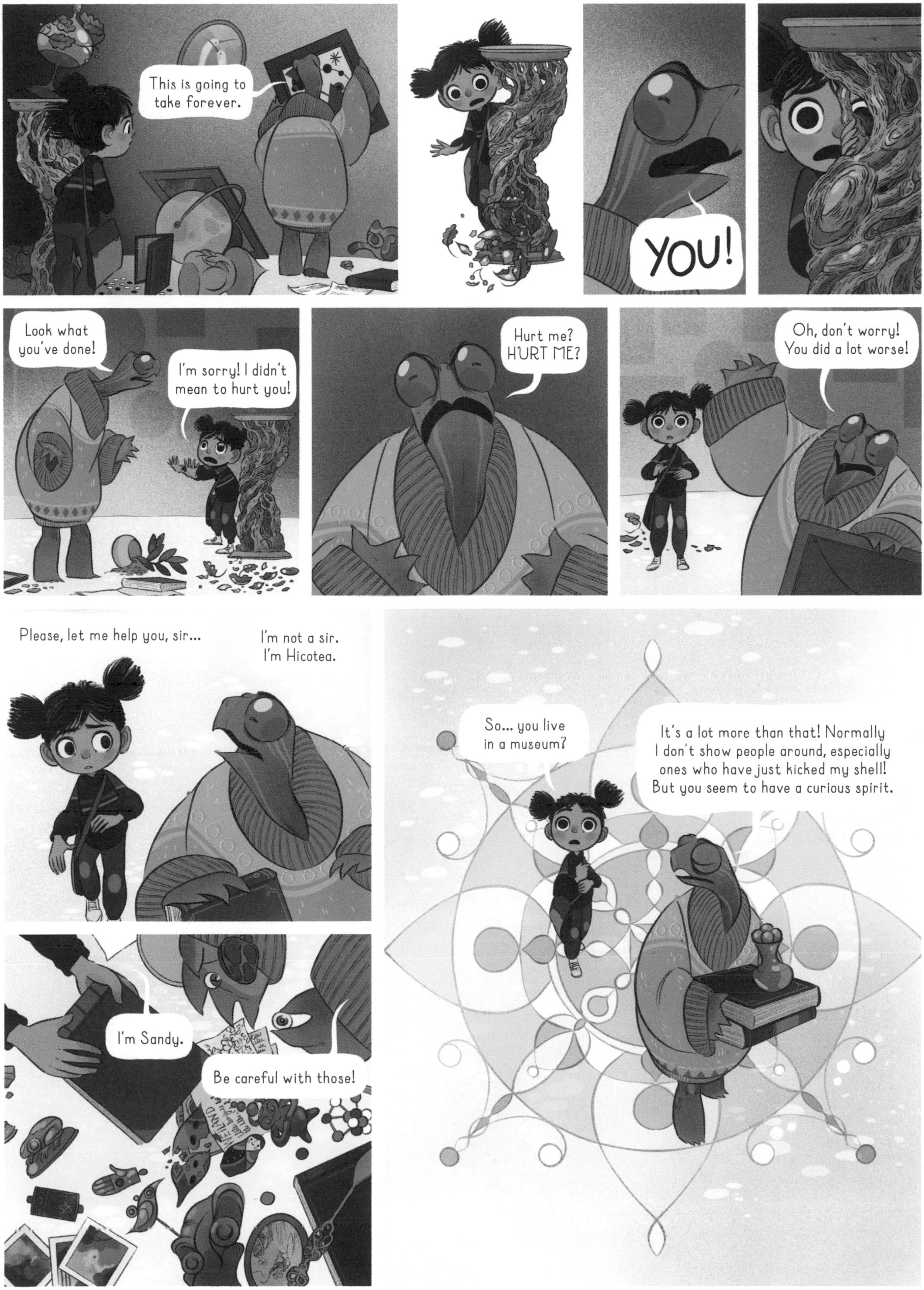
This is going to take forever.
YOU!
Look what you've done!
I'm sorry! I didn't mean to hurt you!
Hurt me? HURT ME?
Oh, don't worry! You did a lot worse!
Please, let me help you, sir...
I'm not a sir. I'm Hicotea.
I'm Sandy.
Be careful with those!
So... you live in a museum?
It's a lot more than that! Normally I don't show people around, especially ones who have just kicked my shell! But you seem to have a curious spirit.

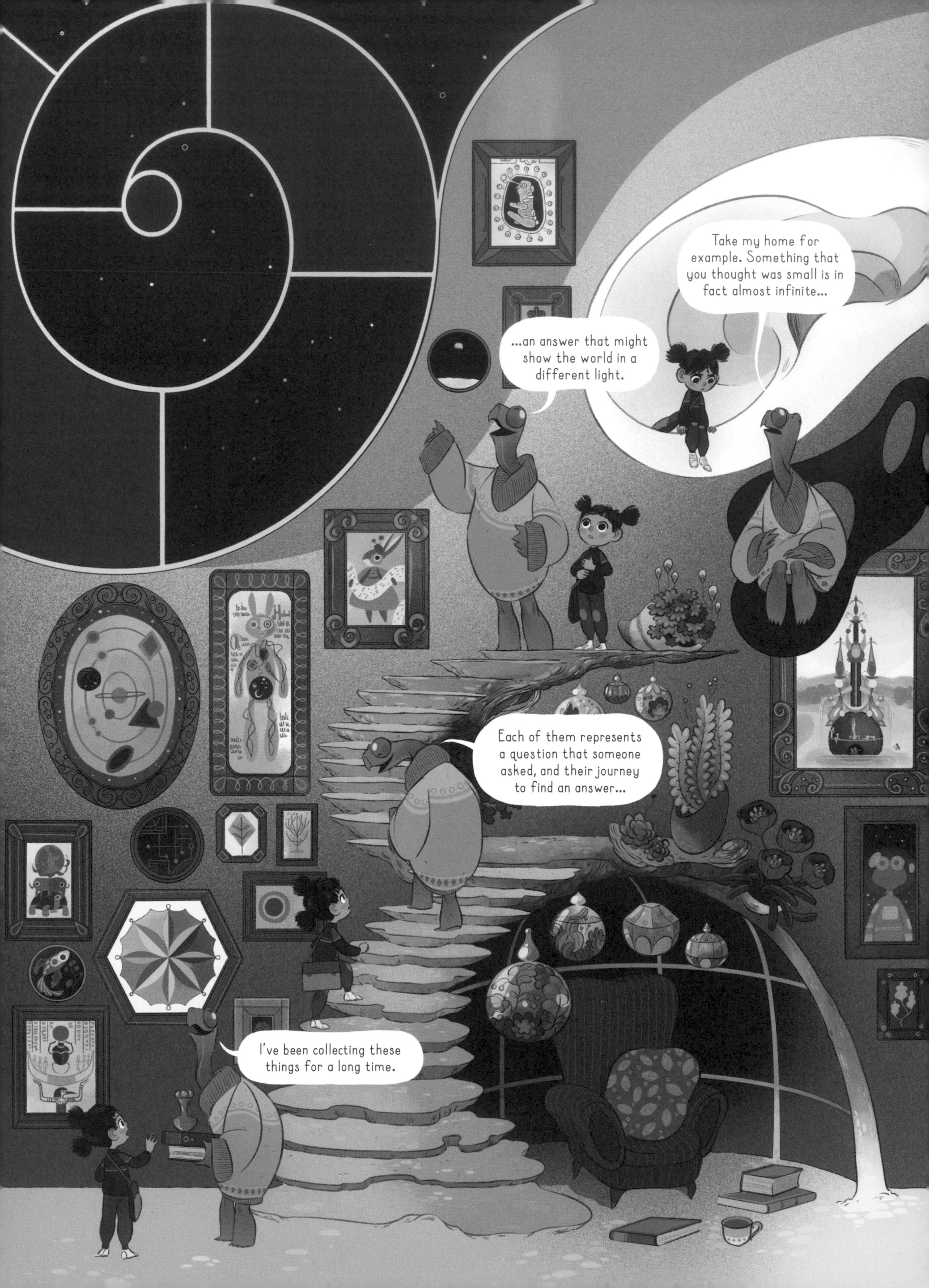
Take my home for example. Something that you thought was small is in fact almost infinite...
...an answer that might show the world in a different light.
Each of them represents a question that someone asked, and their journey to find an answer...
I've been collecting these things for a long time.

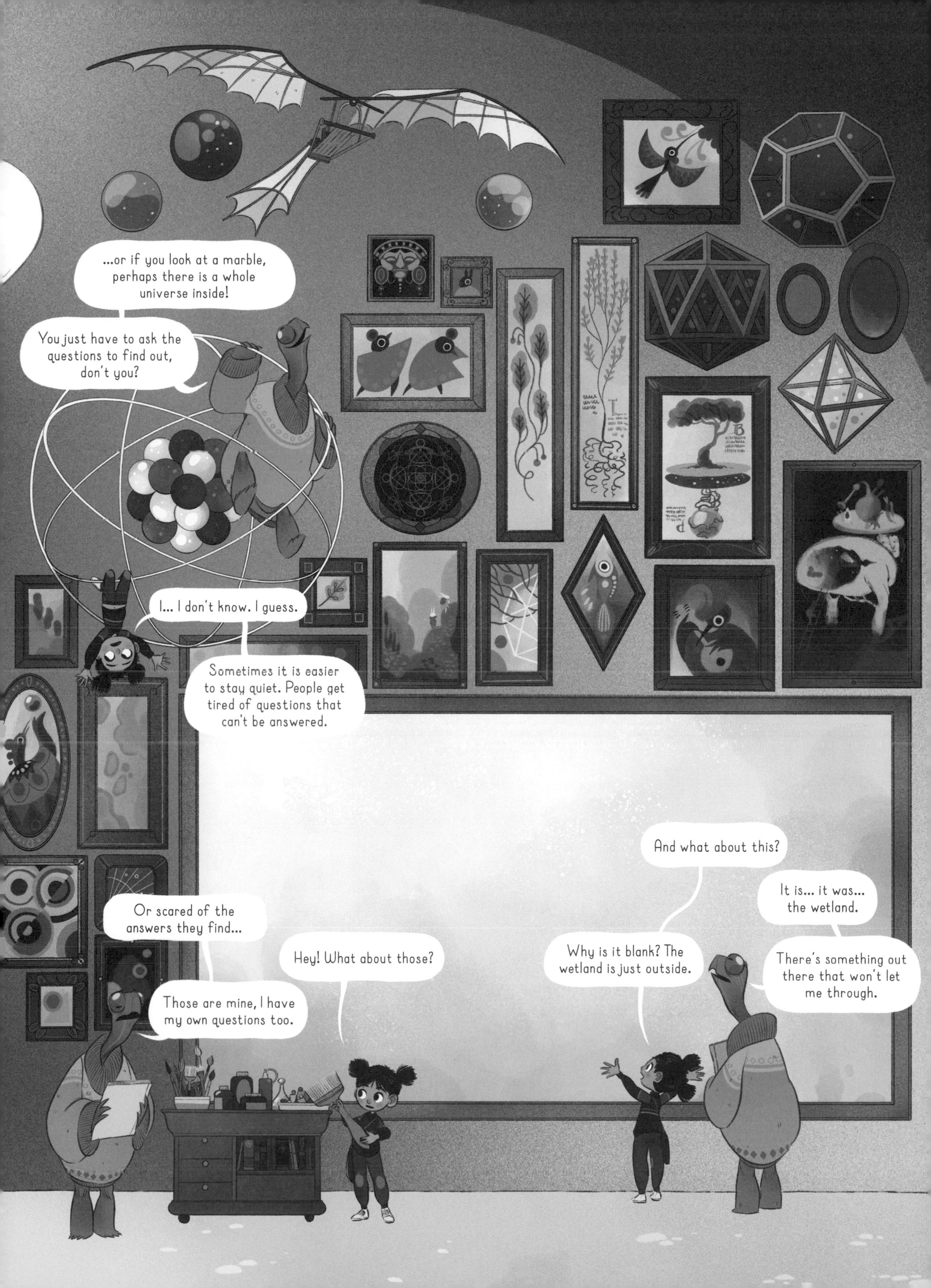
...or if you look at a marble, perhaps there is a whole universe inside!
You just have to ask the questions to find out, don't you?
I... I don't know. I guess.
Sometimes it is easier to stay quiet. People get tired of questions that can't be answered.
Or scared of the answers they find...
Hey! What about those?
Those are mine, I have my own questions too.
And what about this?
It is... it was... the wetland.
Why is it blank? The wetland is just outside.
There's something out there that won't let me through.

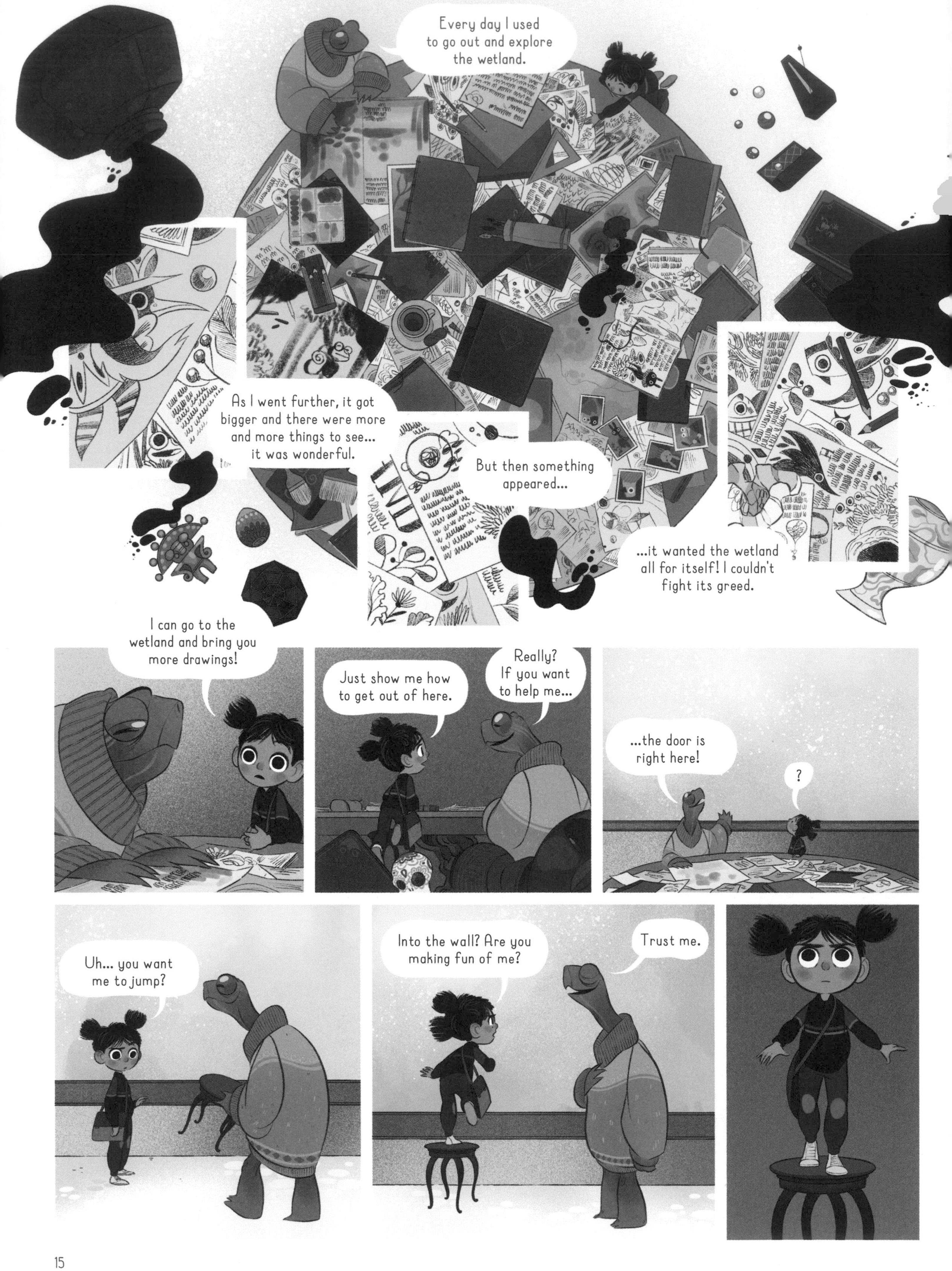
Every day I used to go out and explore the wetland.
As I went further, it got bigger and there were more and more things to see... it was wonderful.
But then something appeared...
...it wanted the wetland all for itself! I couldn't fight its greed.
I can go to the wetland and bring you more drawings!
Just show me how to get out of here.
Really? If you want to help me...
...the door is right here!
?
Uh... you want me to jump?
Into the wall? Are you making fun of me?
Trust me.

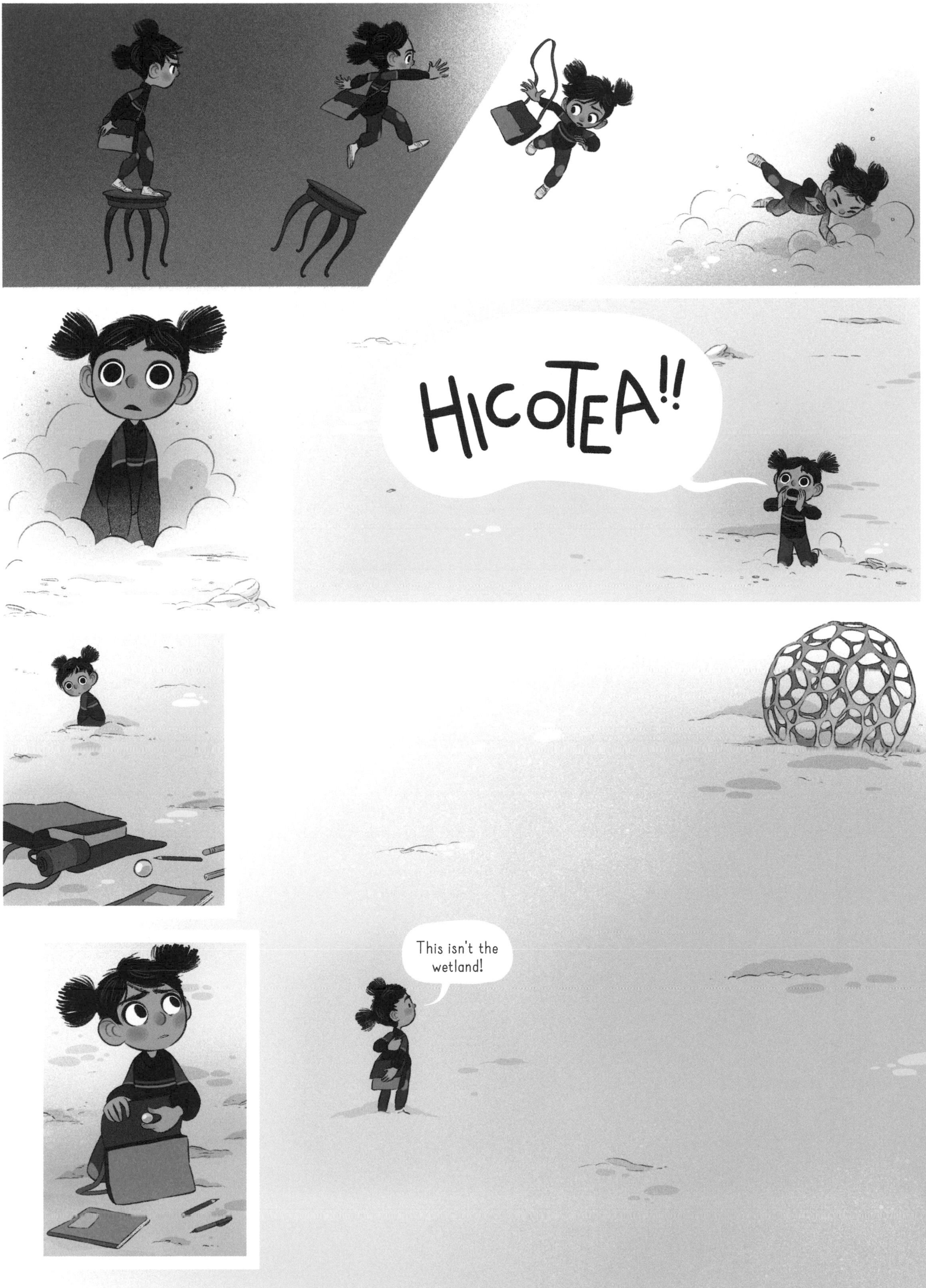
HICOTEA!!
This isn't the wetland!

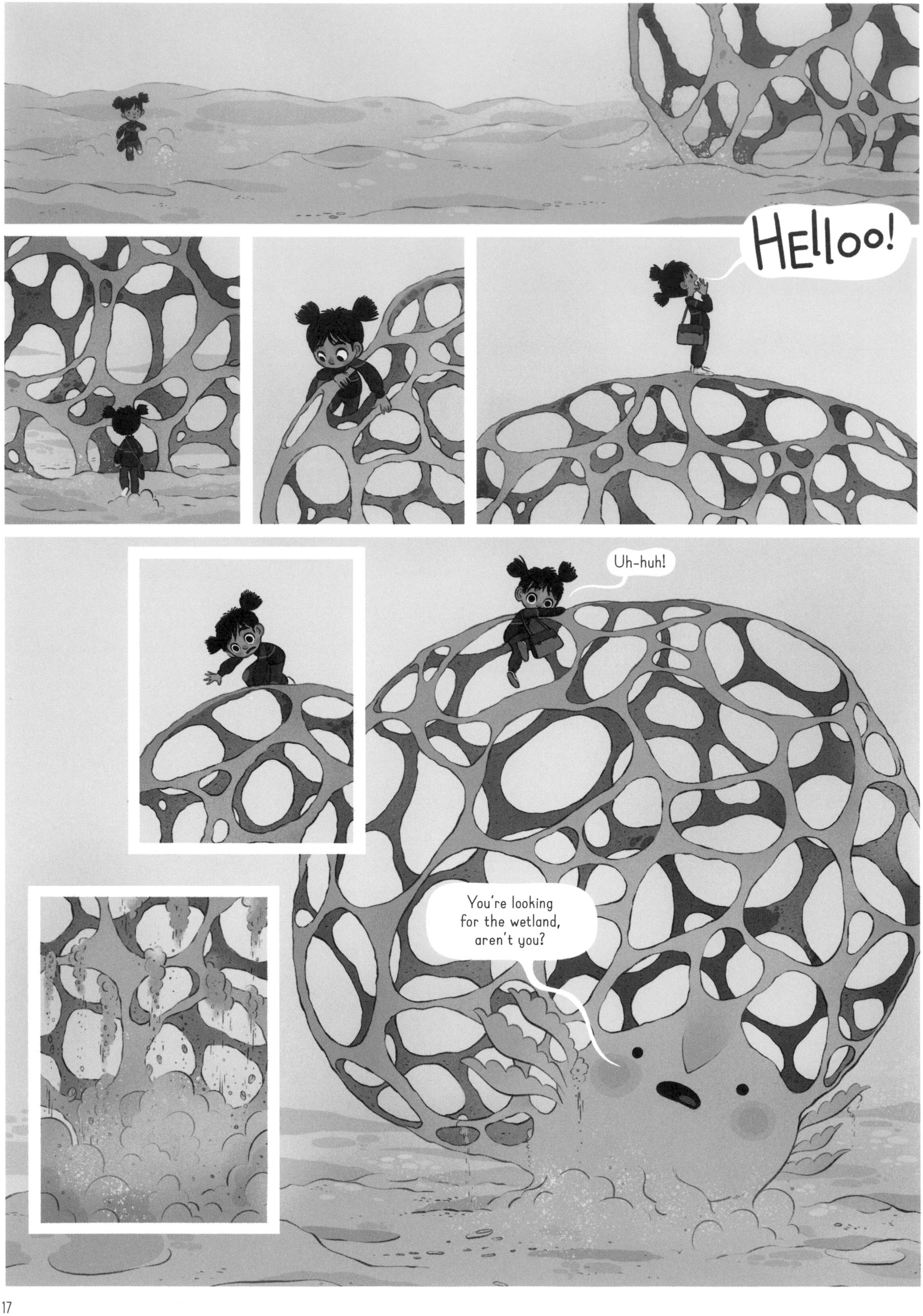
HElloo!
Uh-huh!
You're looking
for the wetland,
aren't you?

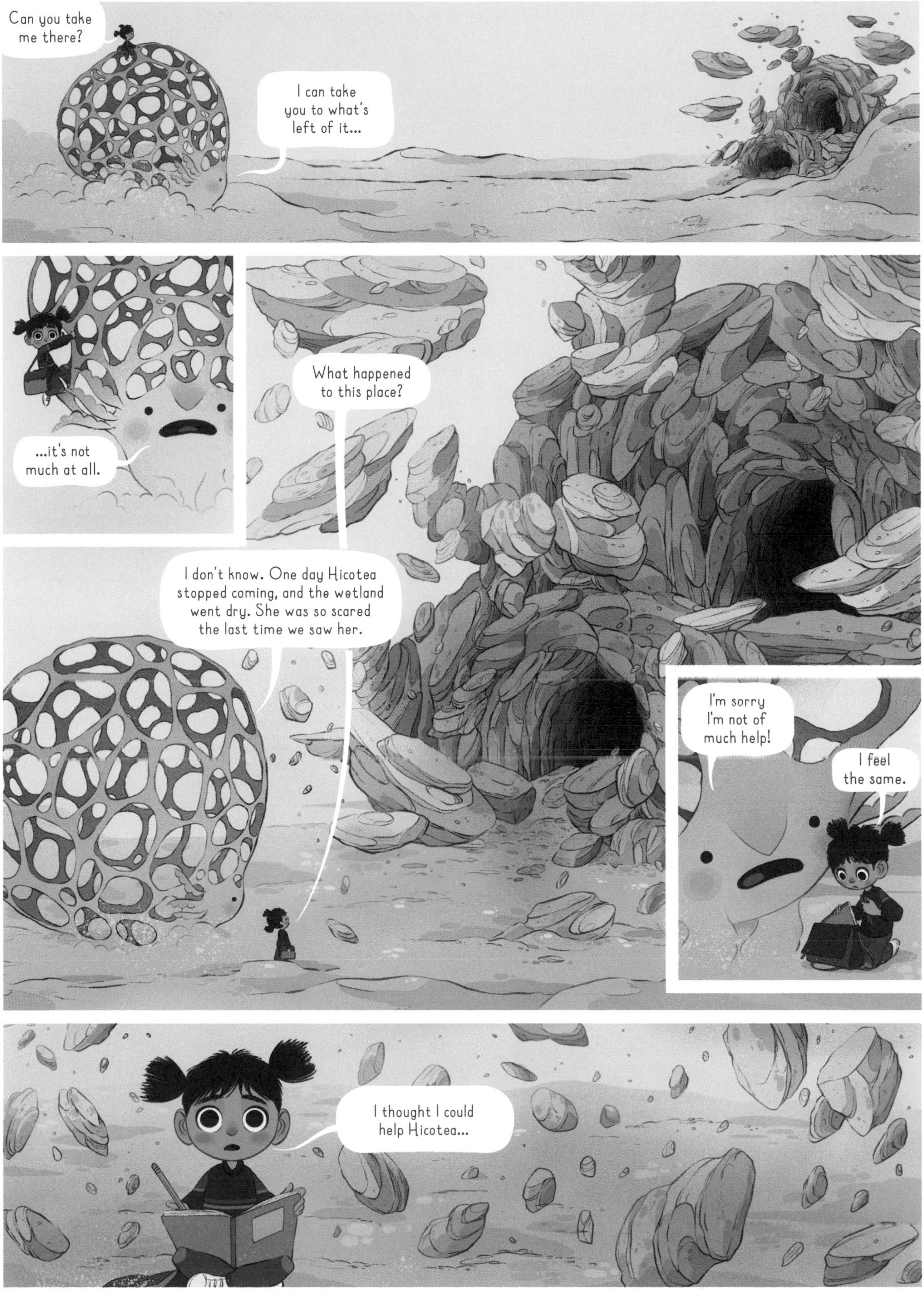
Can you take me there?
I can take you to what's left of it...
...it's not much at all.
What happened to this place?
I don't know. One day Hicotea stopped coming, and the wetland went dry. She was so scared the last time we saw her.
I'm sorry I'm not of much help!
I feel the same.
I thought I could help Hicotea...

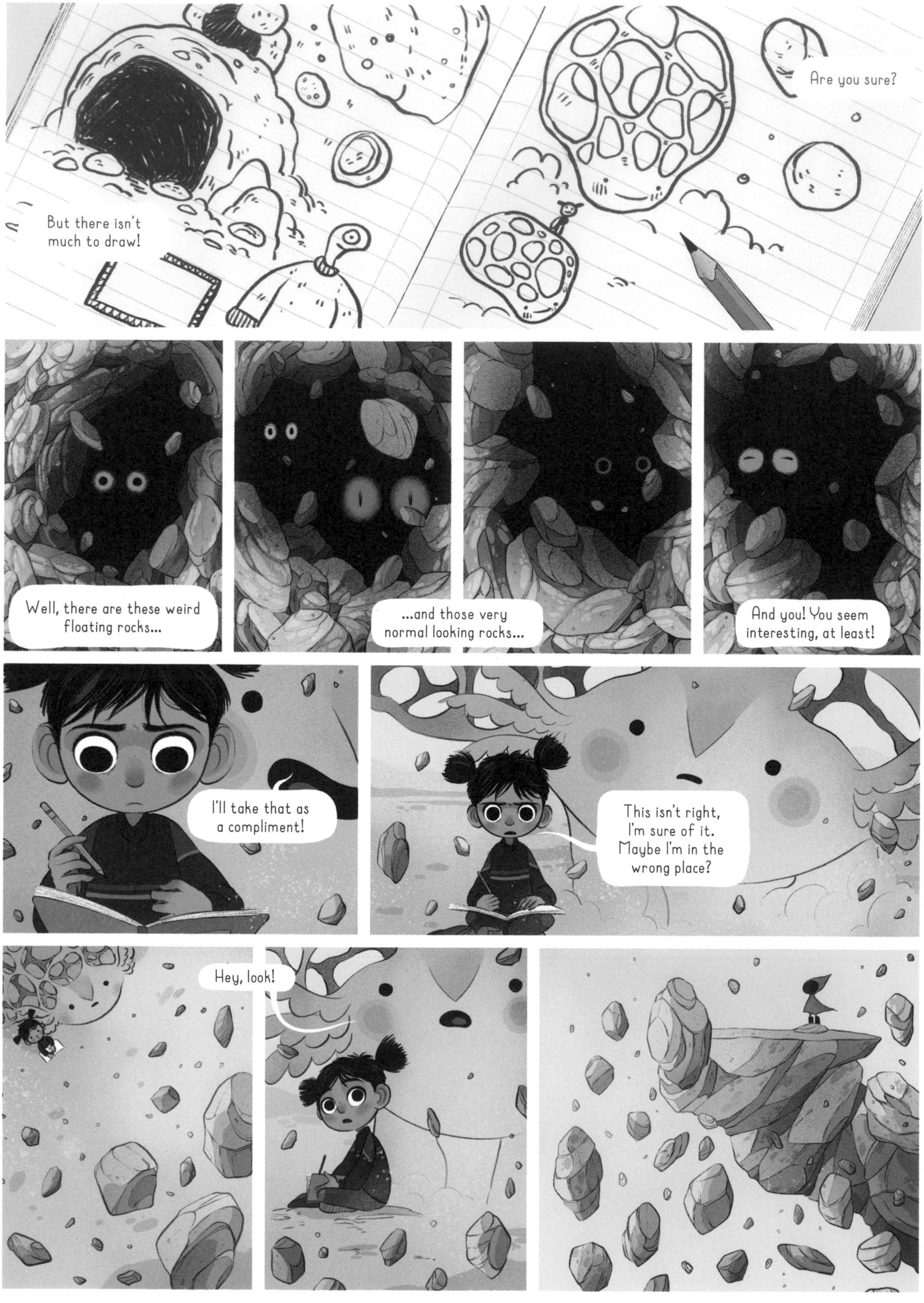
But there isn't much to draw!
Are you sure?
Well, there are these weird floating rocks...
...and those very normal looking rocks...
And you! You seem interesting, at least!
I'll take that as a compliment!
This isn't right, I'm sure of it. Maybe I'm in the wrong place?
Hey, look!

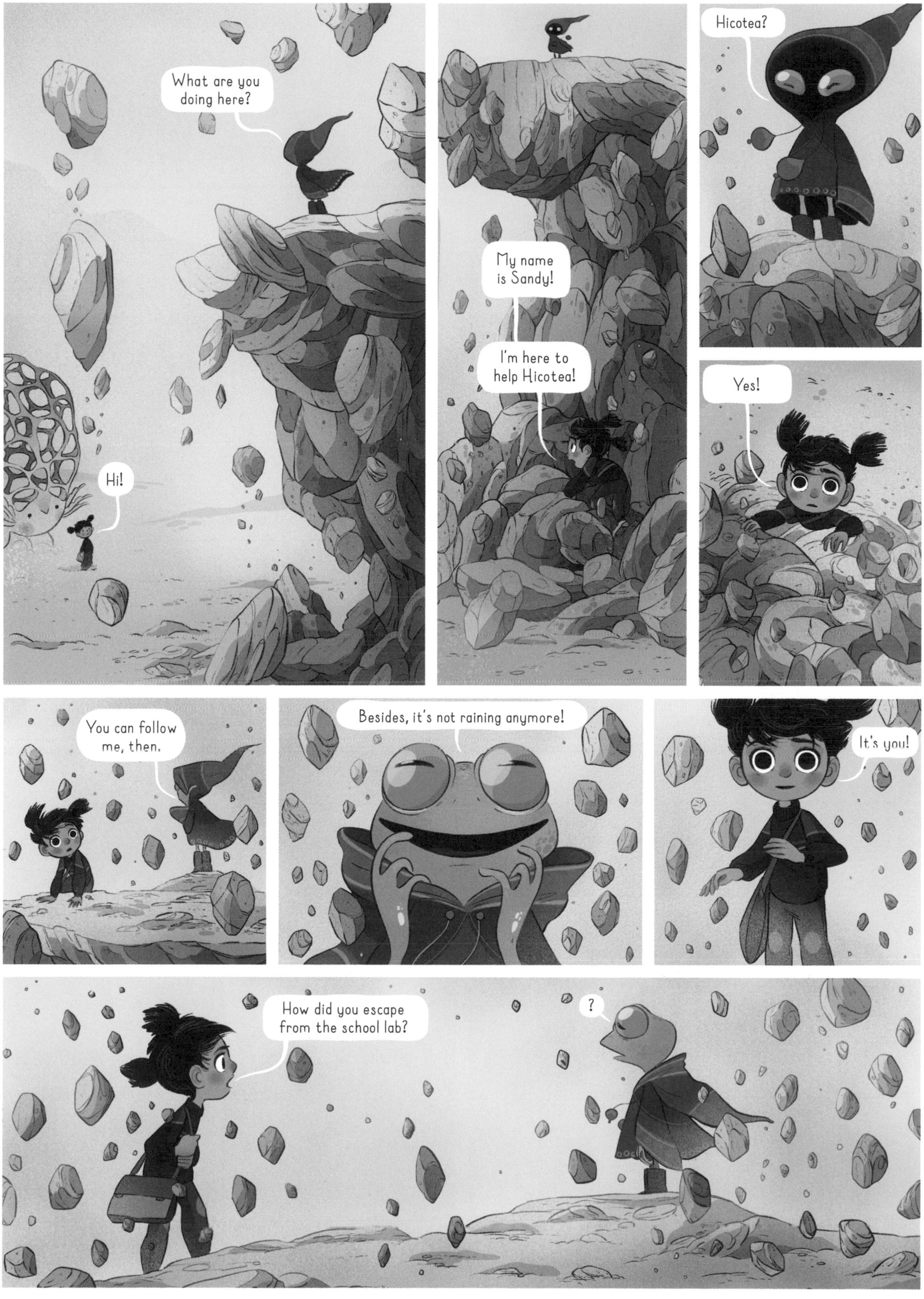
What are you doing here?
Hi!
My name is Sandy!
I'm here to help Hicotea!
Hicotea?
Yes!
You can follow me, then.
Besides, it's not raining anymore!
It's you!
How did you escape from the school lab?
?

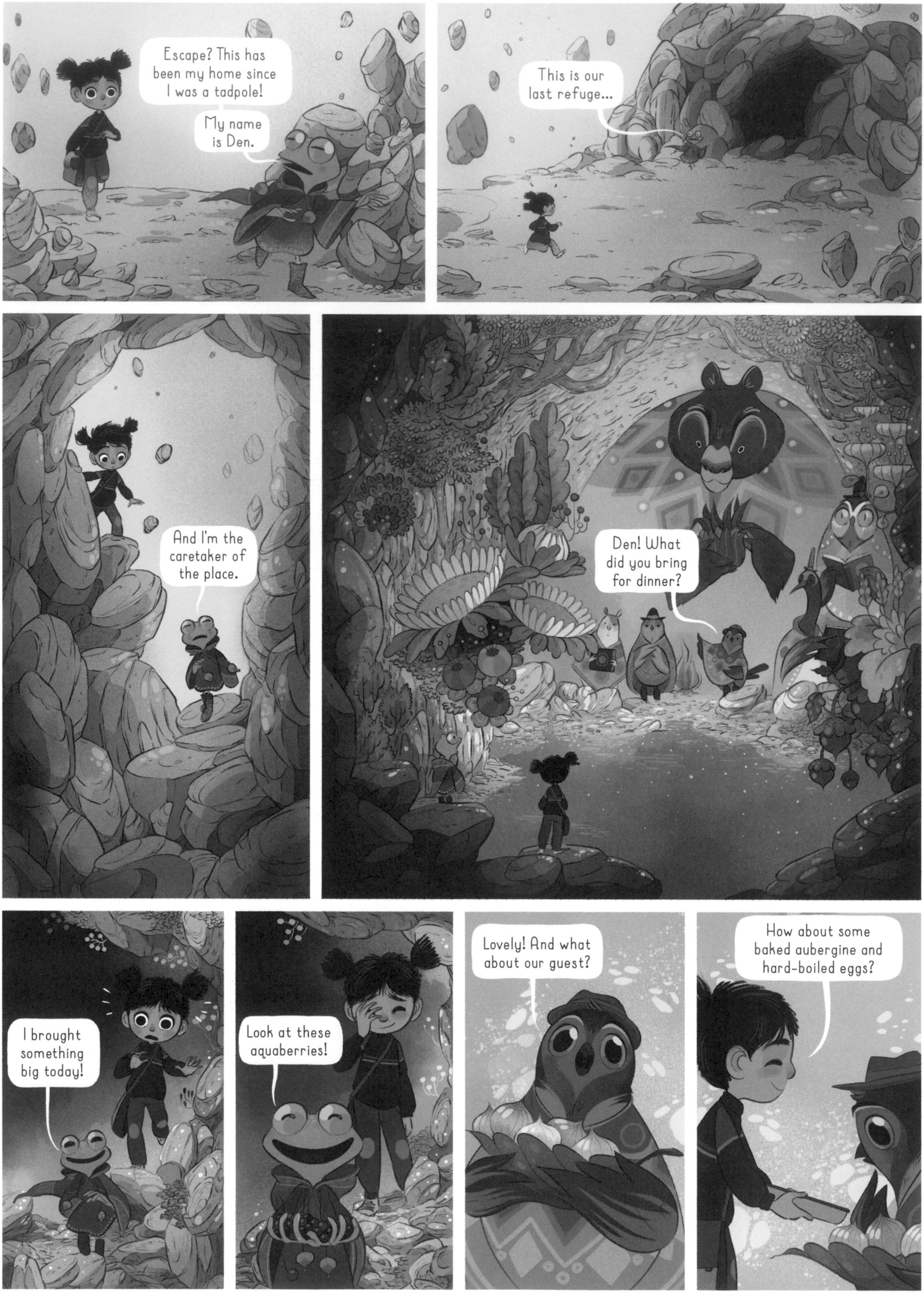
Escape? This has been my home since I was a tadpole!
My name is Den.
This is our last refuge...
And I'm the caretaker of the place.
Den! What did you bring for dinner?
I brought something big today!
Look at these aquaberries!
Lovely! And what about our guest?
How about some baked aubergine and hard-boiled eggs?

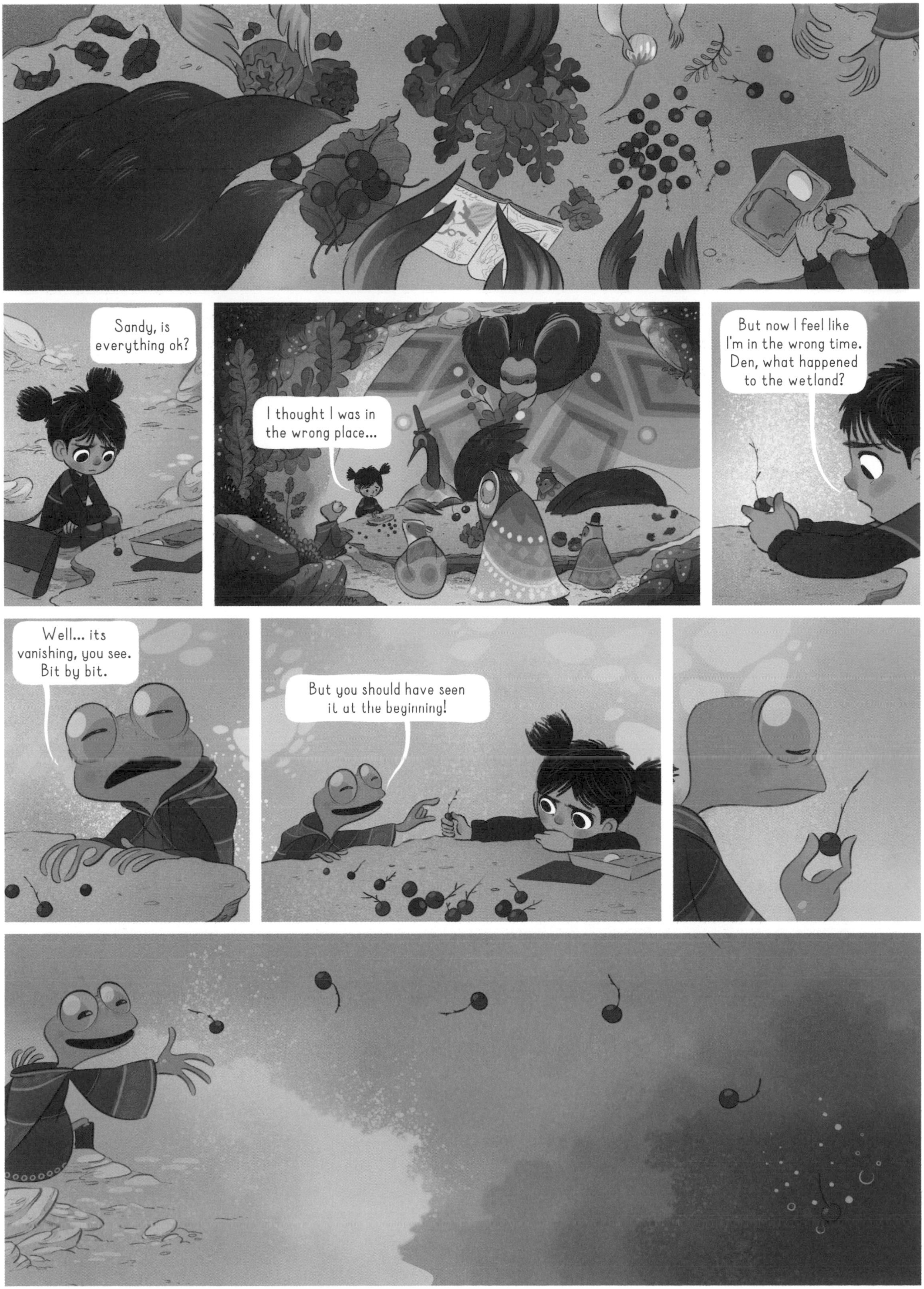
Sandy, is everything ok?
I thought I was in the wrong place...
But now I feel like I'm in the wrong time. Den, what happened to the wetland?
Well... its vanishing, you see. Bit by bit.
But you should have seen it at the beginning!

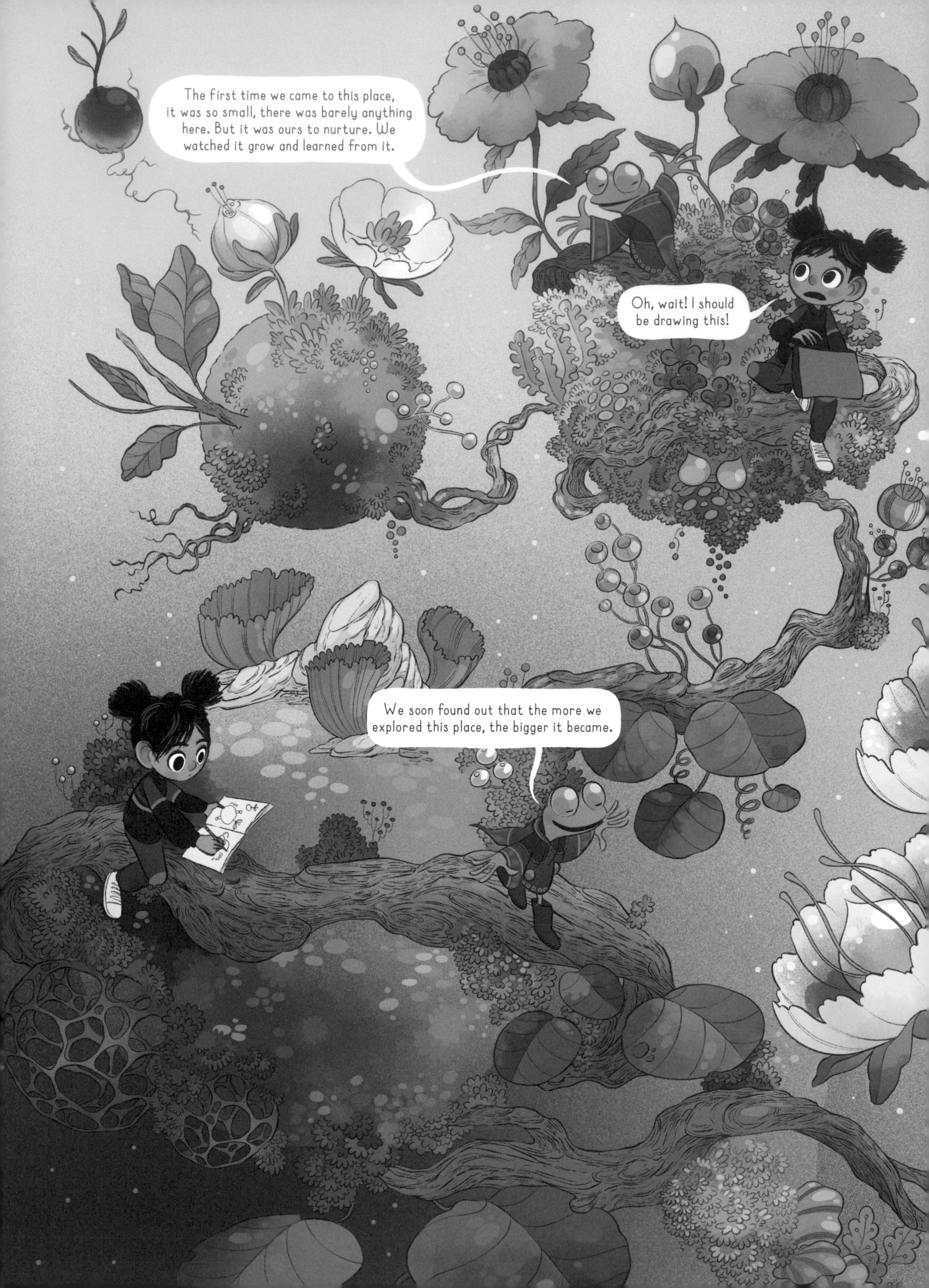
The first time we came to this place, it was so small, there was barely anything here. But it was ours to nurture. We watched it grow and learned from it.
Oh, wait! I should be drawing this!
We soon found out that the more we explored this place, the bigger it became.

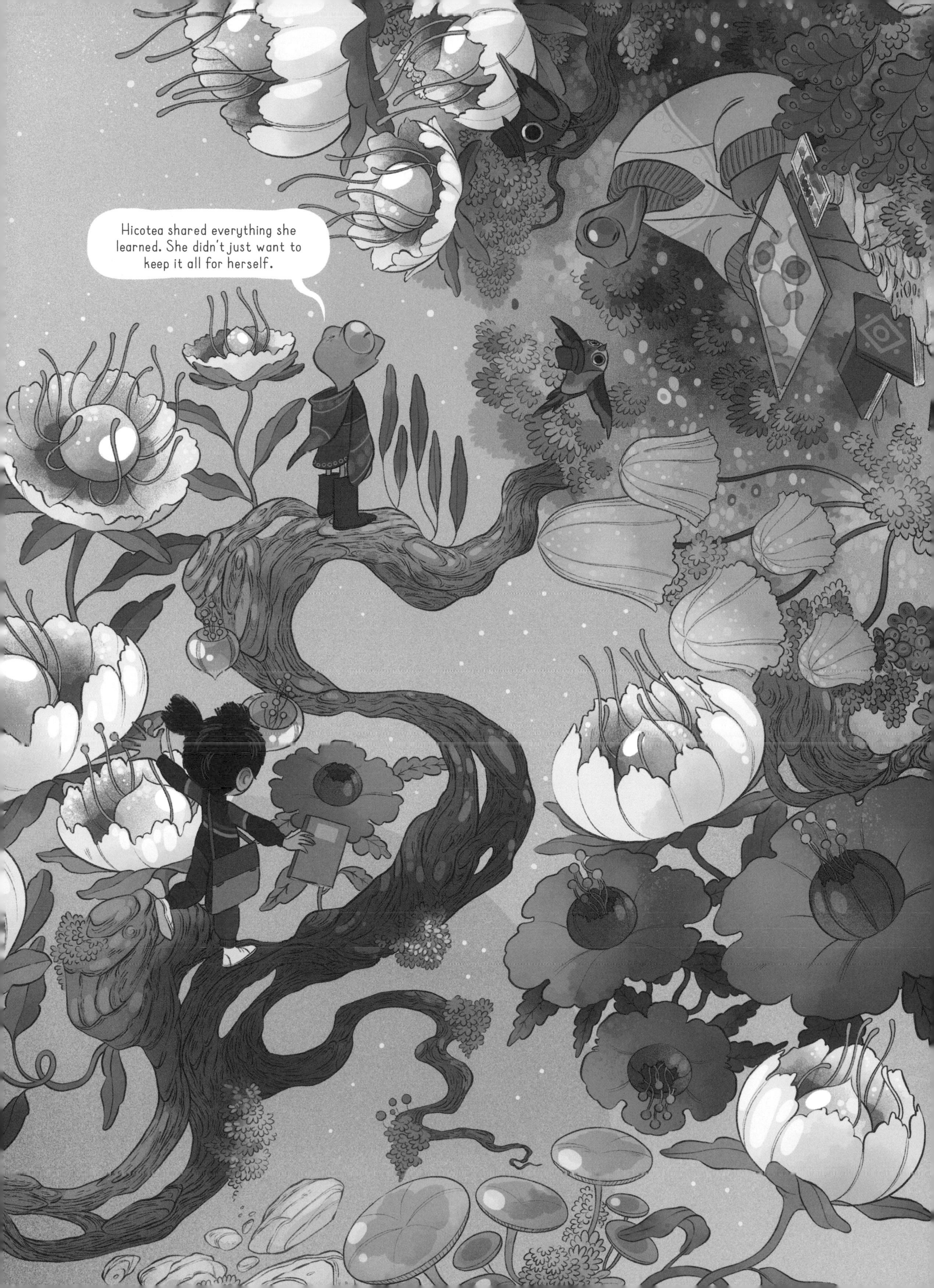
Hicotea shared everything she learned. She didn't just want to keep it all for herself.

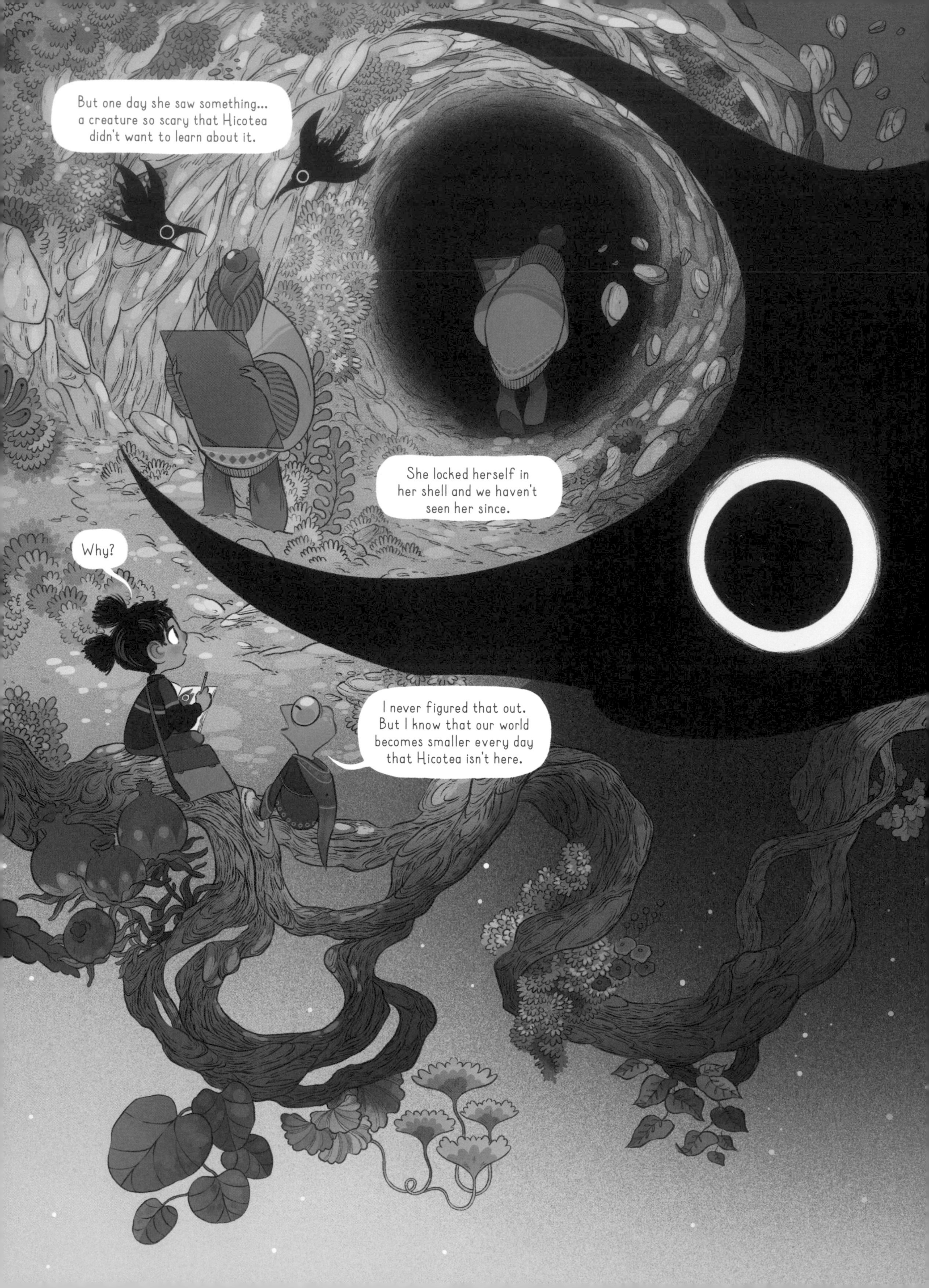
But one day she saw something... a creature so scary that Hicotea didn't want to learn about it.
She locked herself in her shell and we haven't seen her since.
Why?
I never figured that out. But I know that our world becomes smaller every day that Hicotea isn't here.

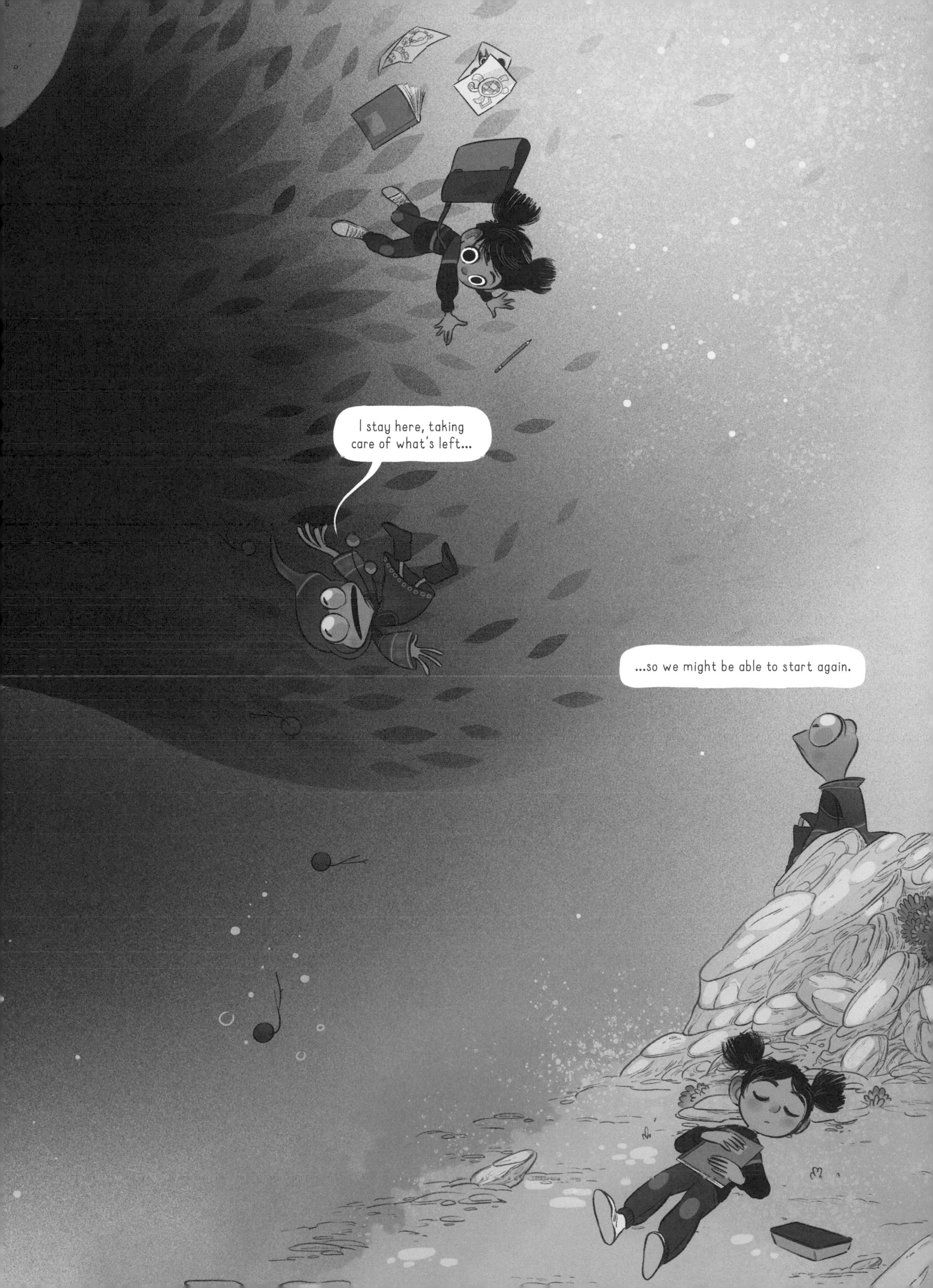
I stay here, taking care of what's left...
...so we might be able to start again.

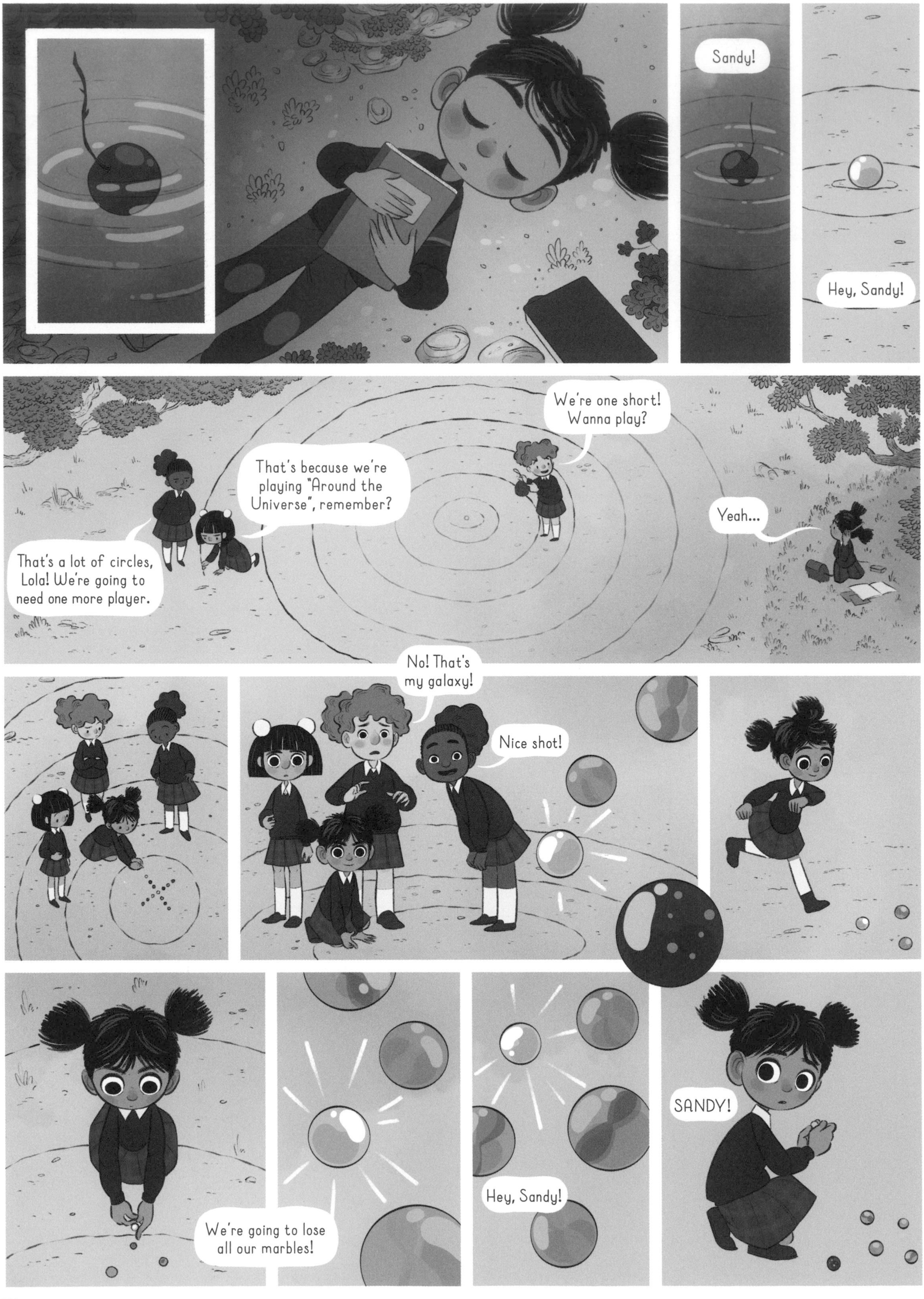

Sandy!
Hey, Sandy!
We're one short! Wanna play?
That's because we're playing "Around the Universe", remember?
That's a lot of circles, Lola! We're going to need one more player.
Yeah...
No! That's my galaxy!
Nice shot!
We're going to lose all our marbles!
Hey, Sandy!
SANDY!

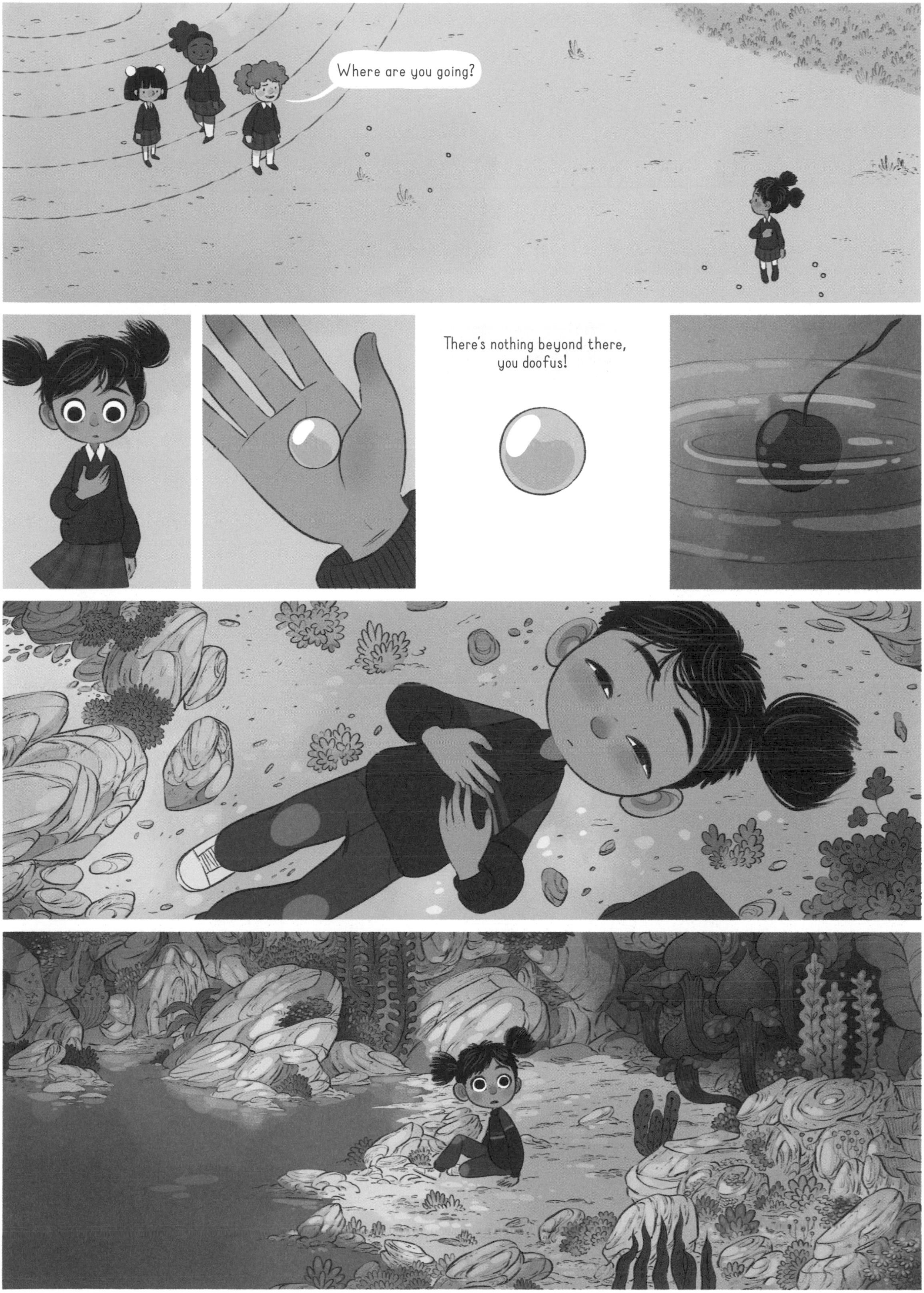
Where are you going?
There's nothing beyond there, you doofus!

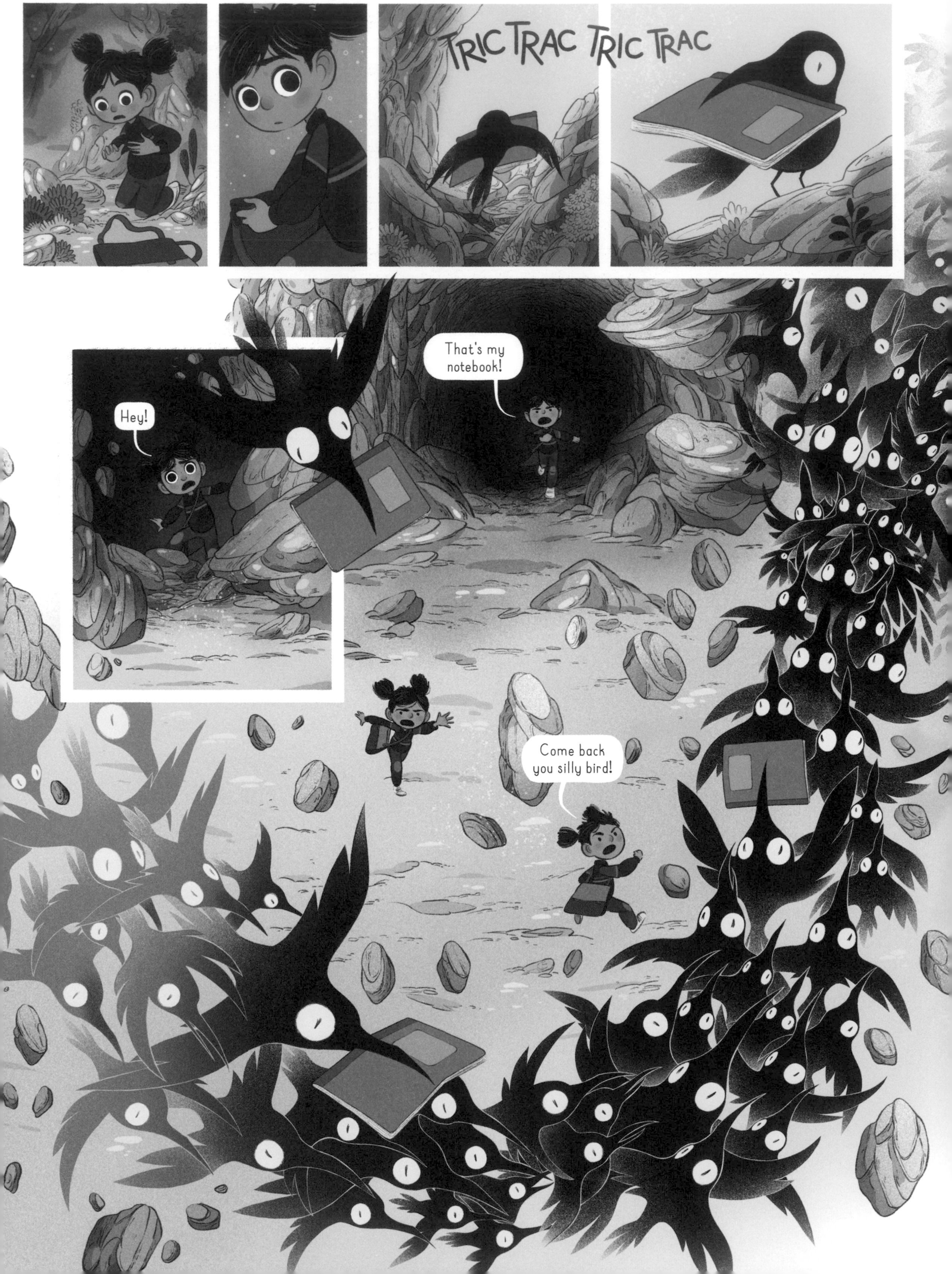

TRIC TRAC TRIC TRAC
Hey!
That's my notebook!
Come back you silly bird!

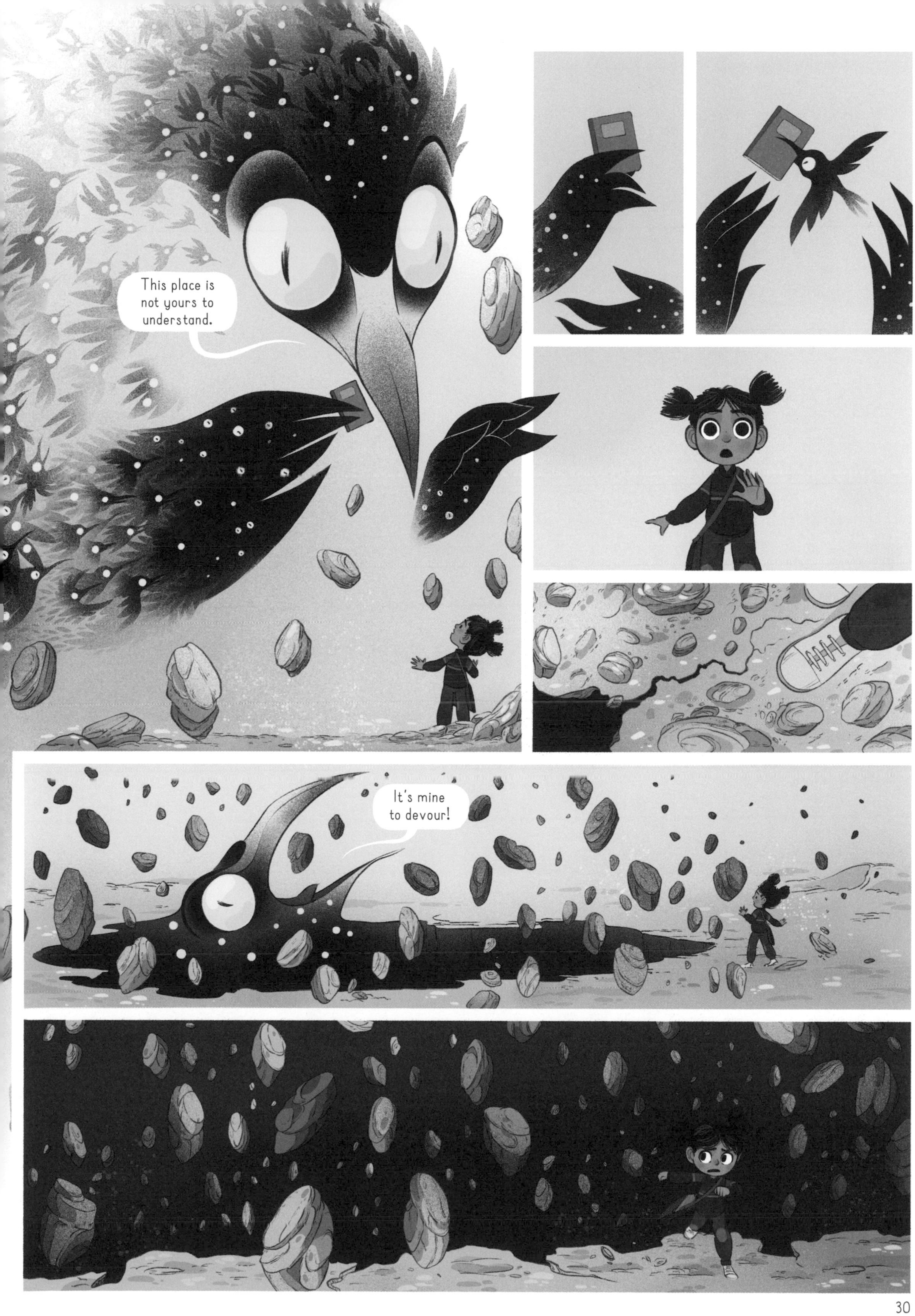
This place is not yours to understand.
It's mine to devour!

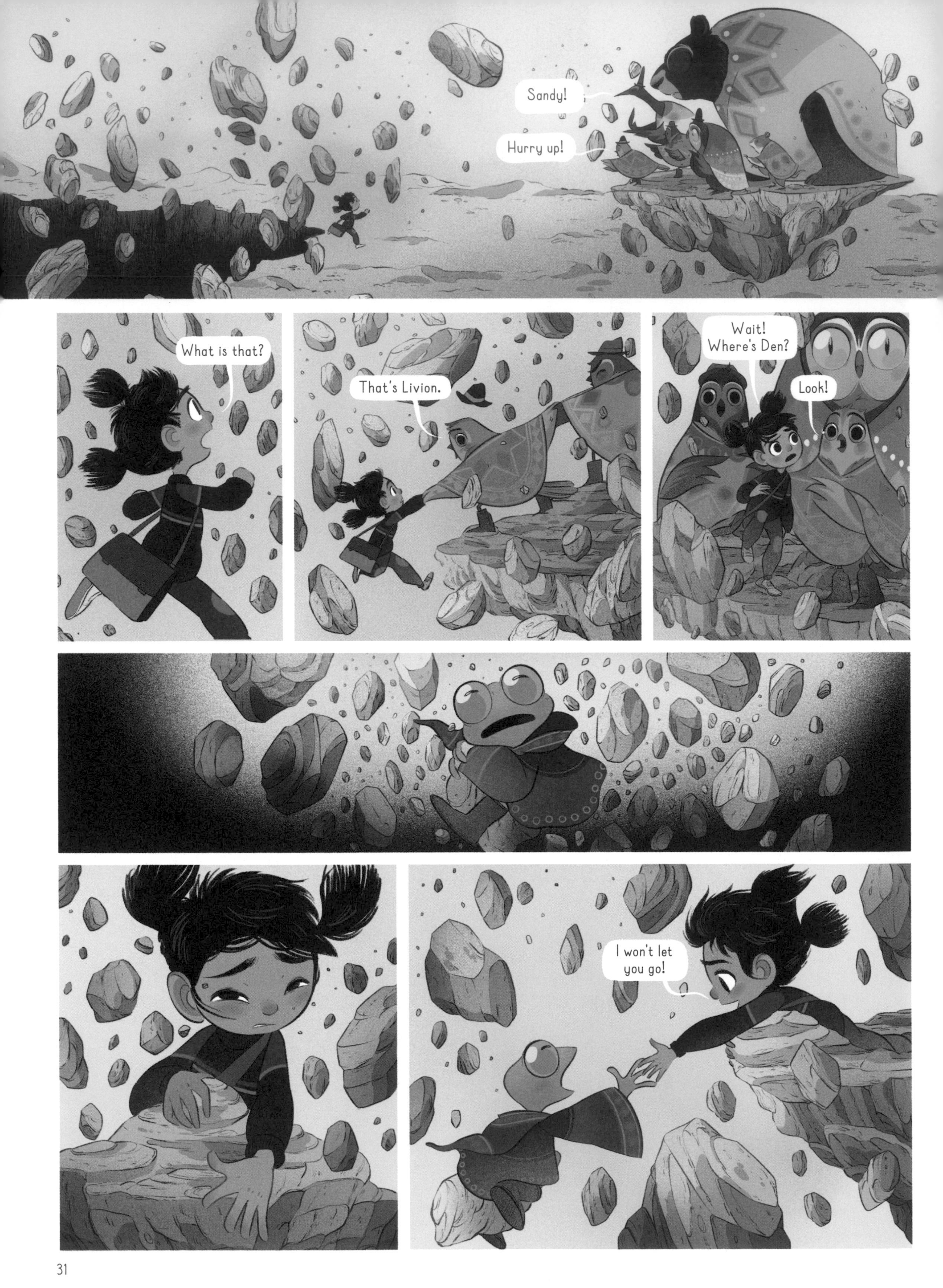
Sandy!
Hurry up!
What is that?
That's Livion.
Wait! Where's Den?
Look!
I won't let you go!

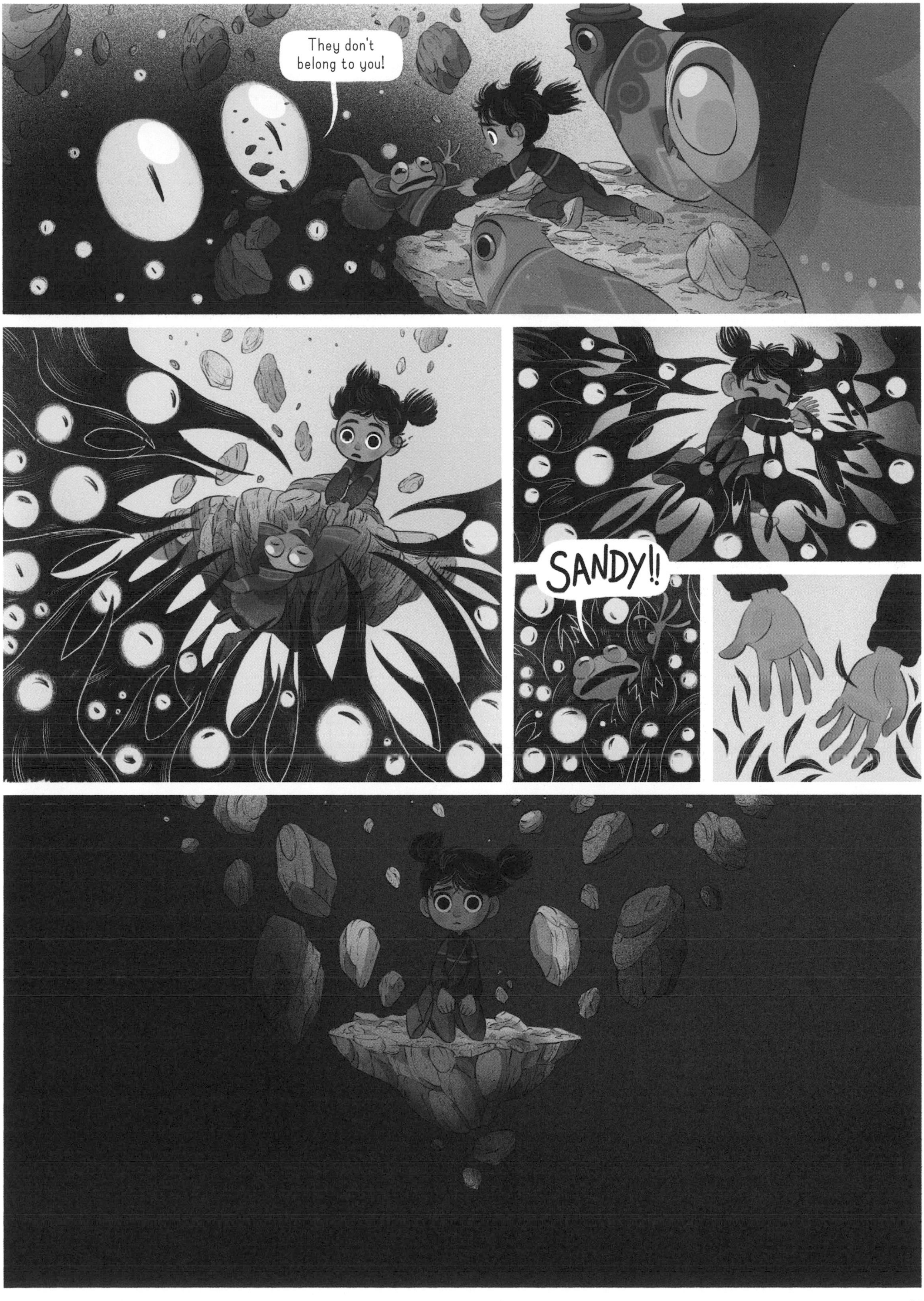
They don't belong to you!
SANDY!!

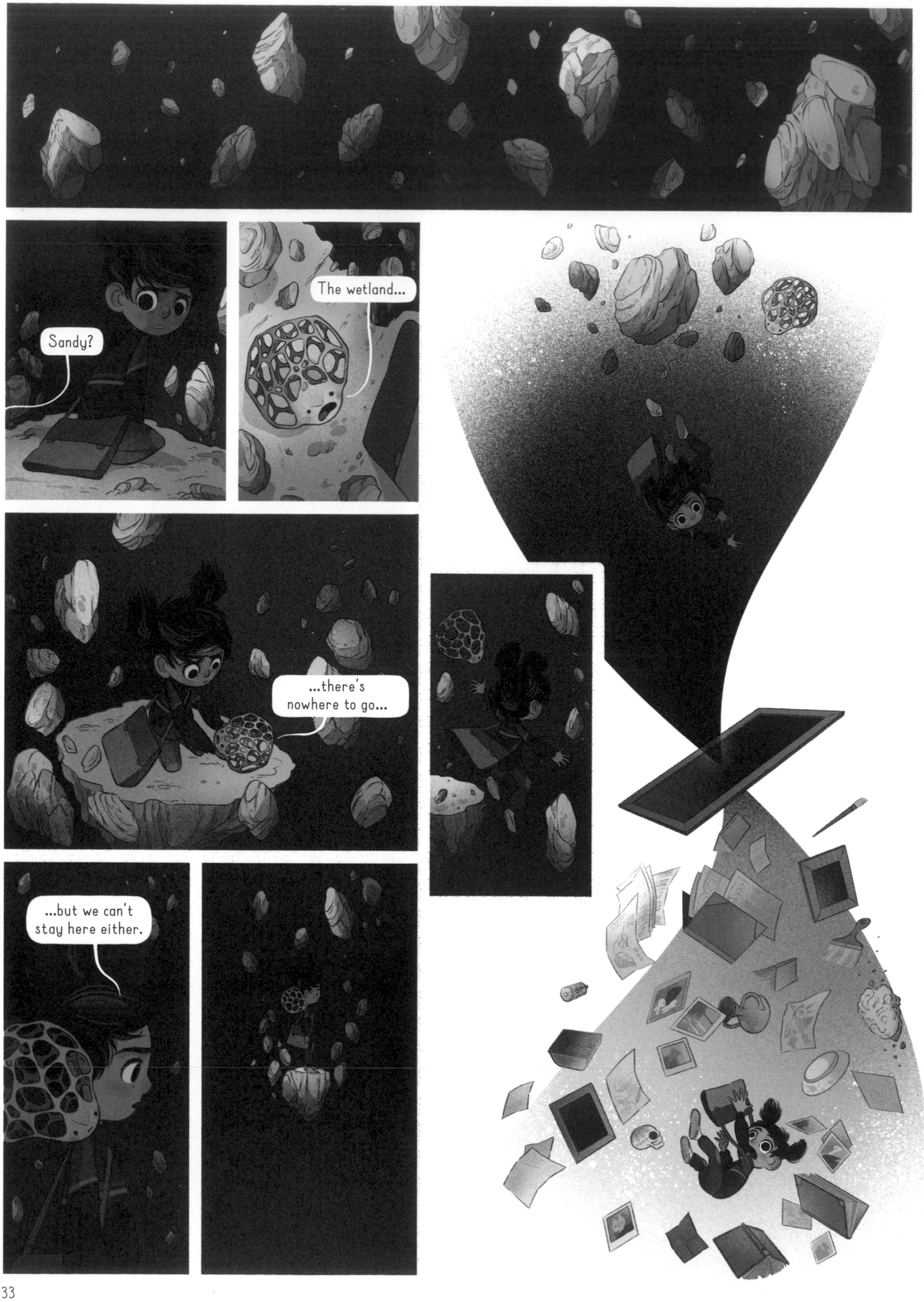
Sandy?
The wetland...
...there's nowhere to go...
...but we can't stay here either.

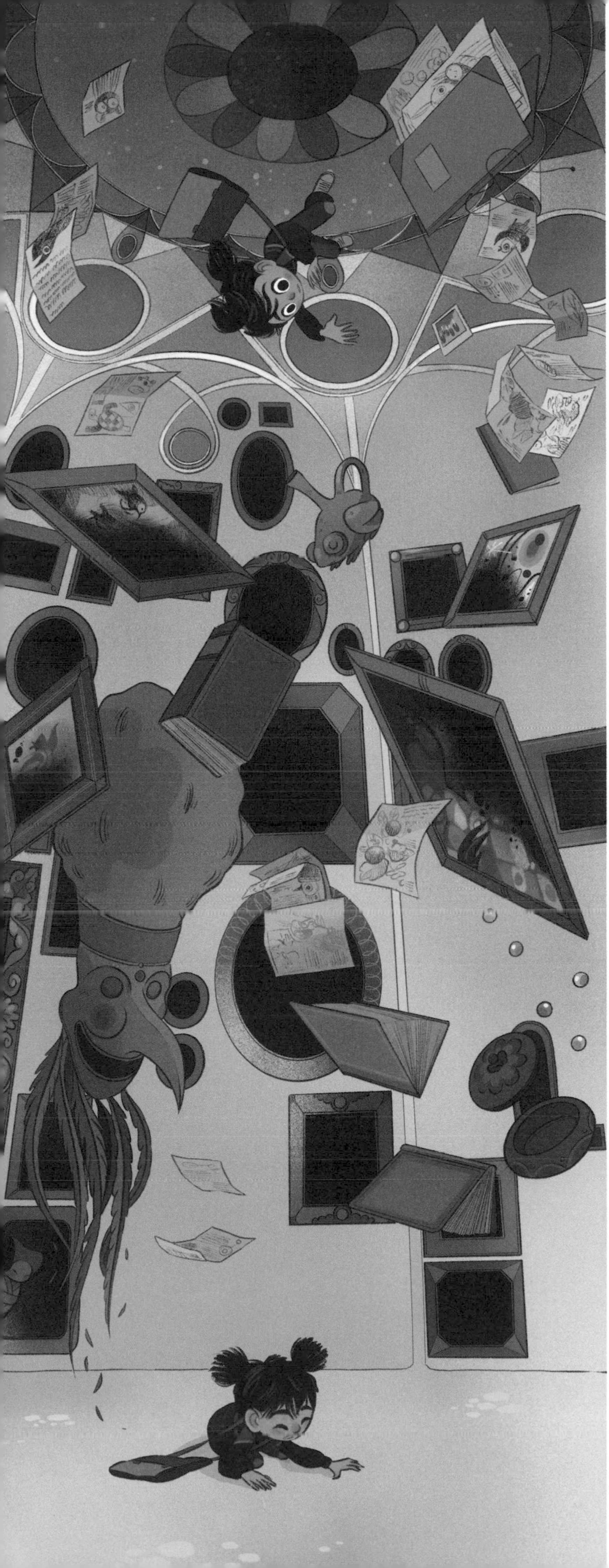

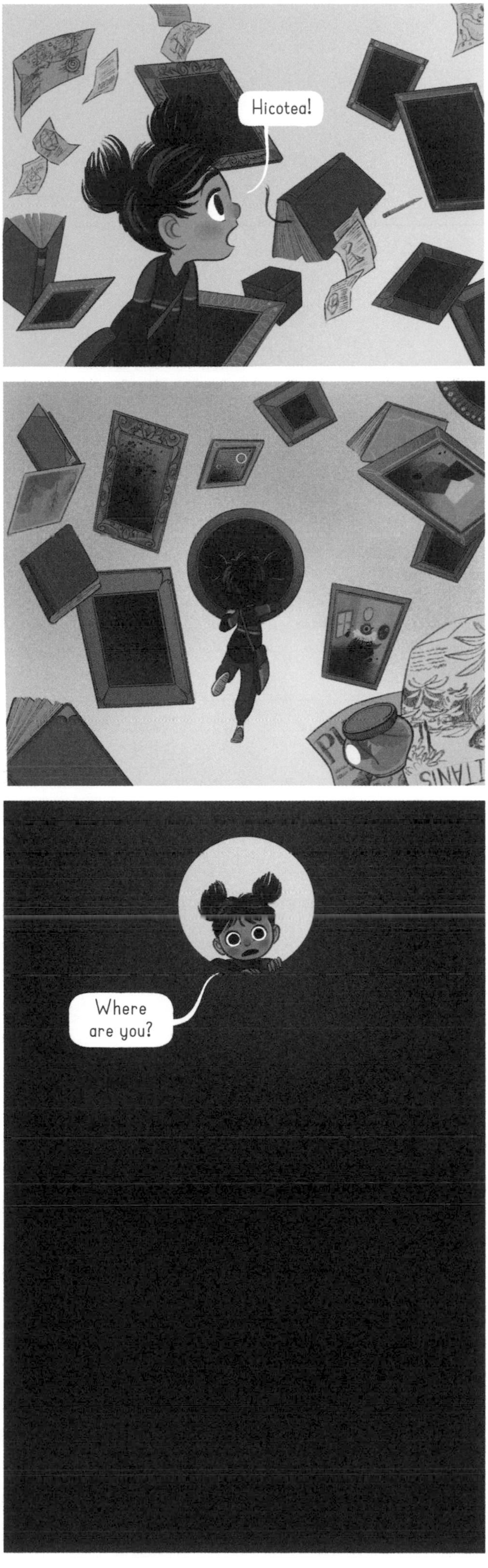
Hicotea!
Where are you?

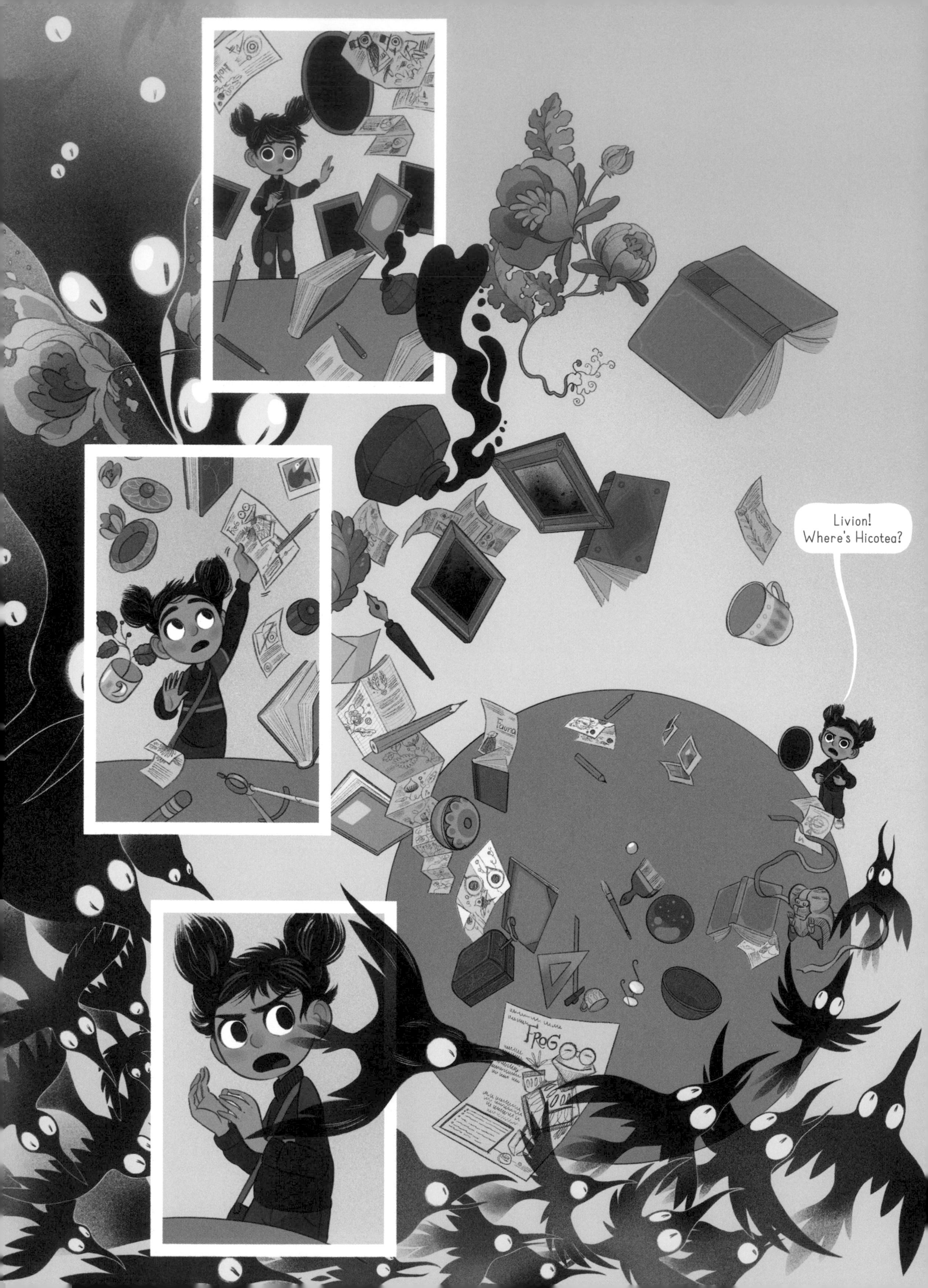
Livion!
Where's Hicotea?
Fauna
FROG

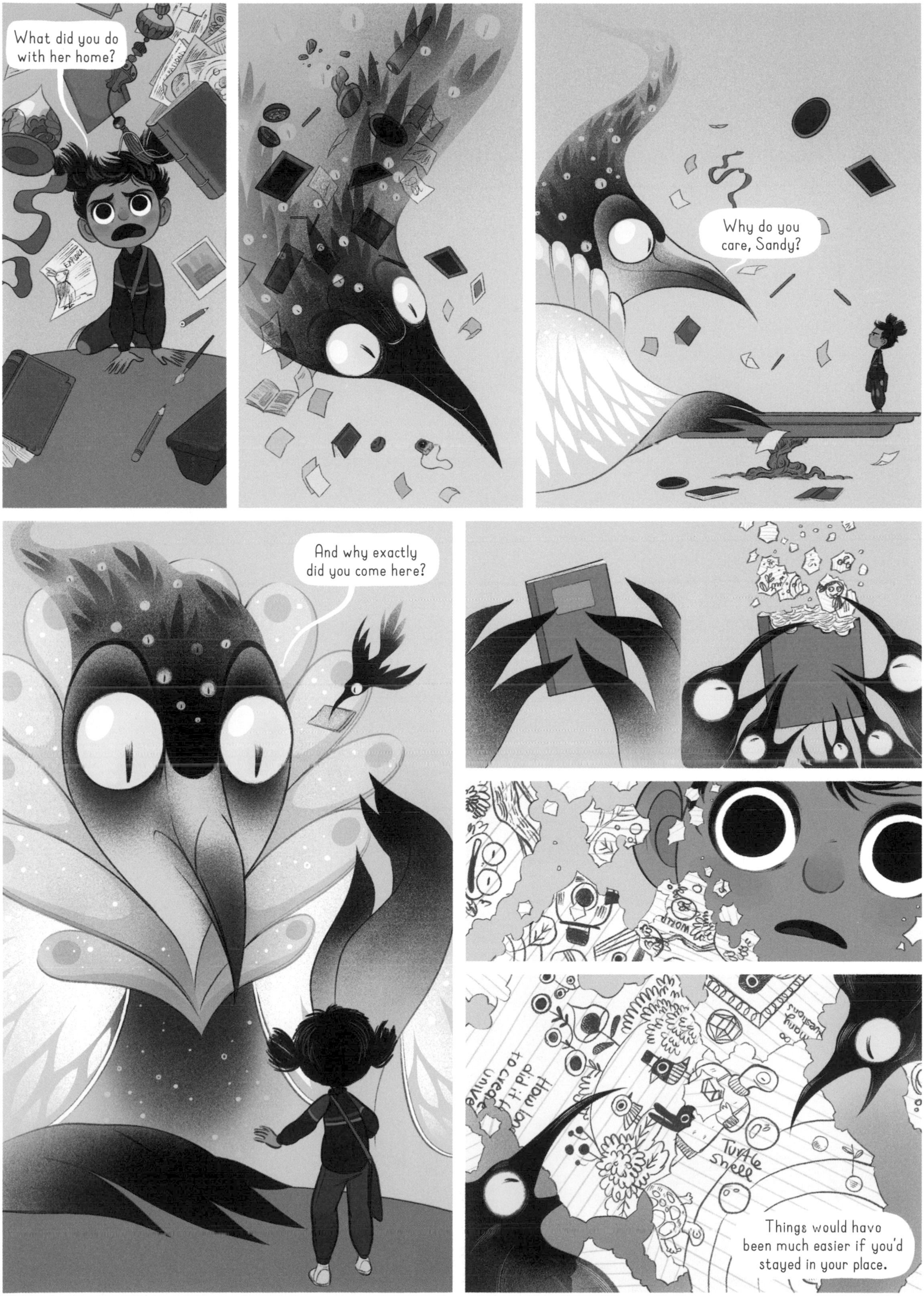
What did you do with her home?
Why do you care, Sandy?
And why exactly did you come here?
Things would have been much easier if you'd stayed in your place.

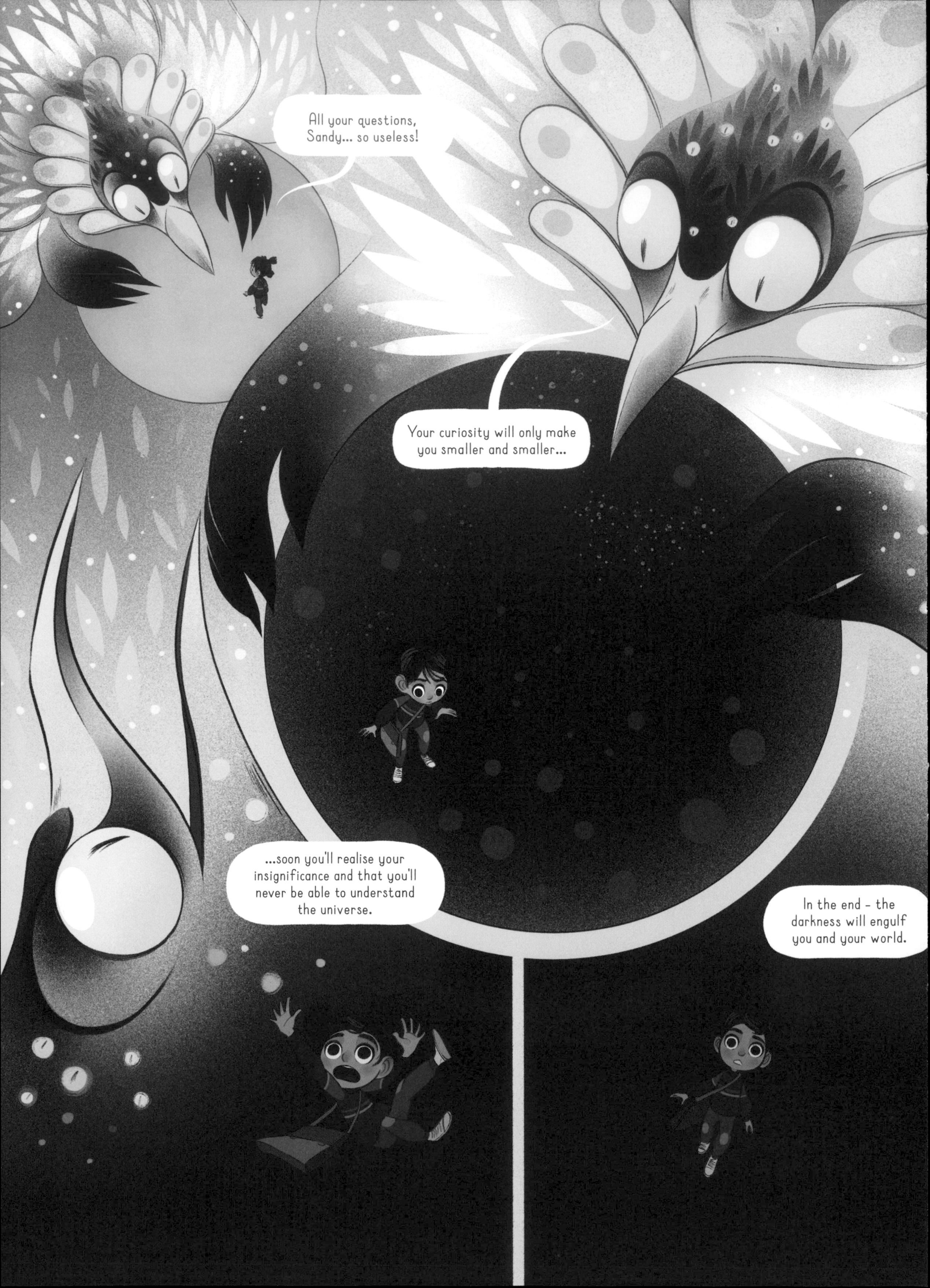
All your questions, Sandy... so useless!
Your curiosity will only make you smaller and smaller...
...soon you'll realise your insignificance and that you'll never be able to understand the universe.
In the end - the darkness will engulf you and your world.

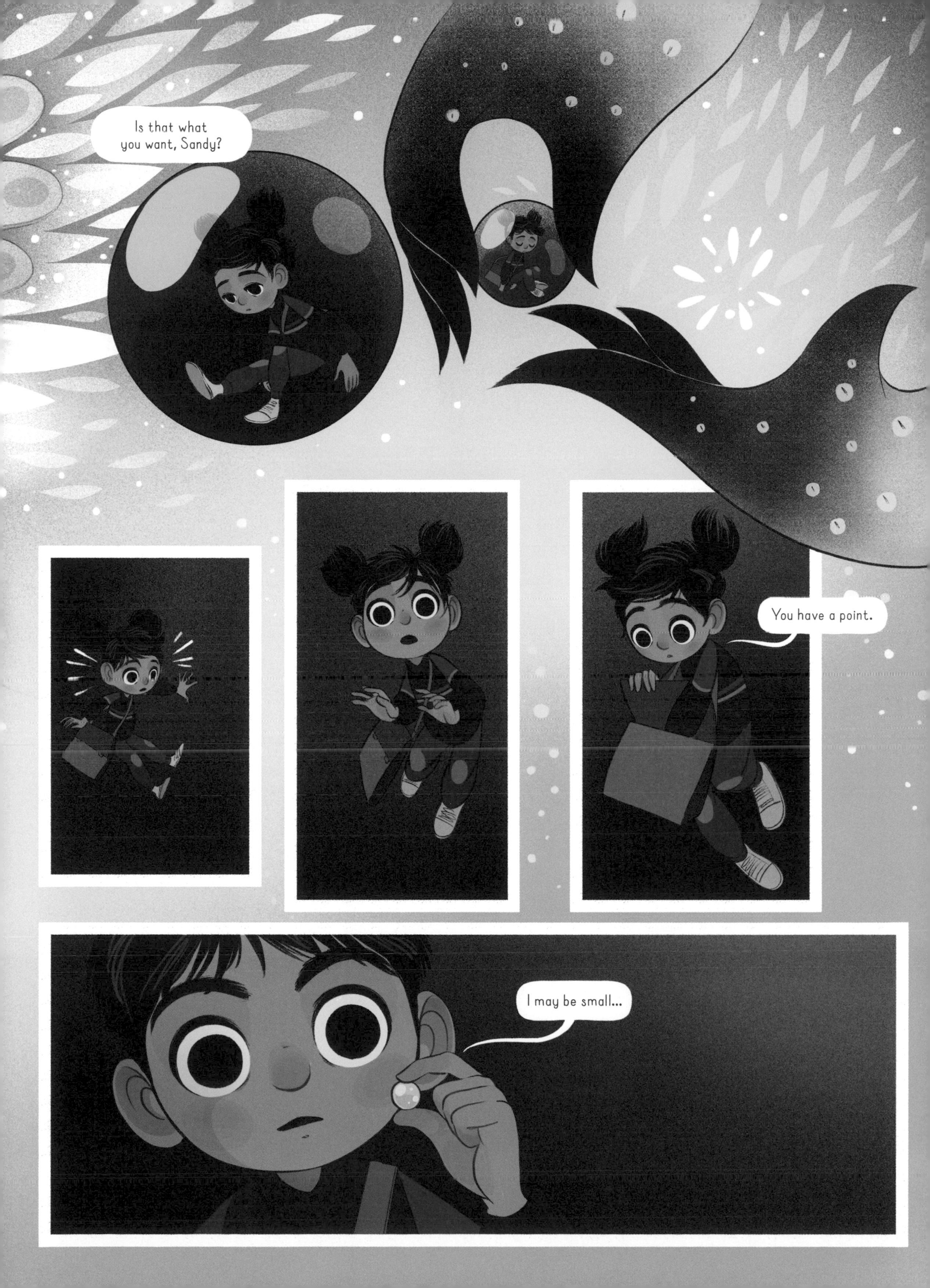
Is that what you want, Sandy?
You have a point.
I may be small...

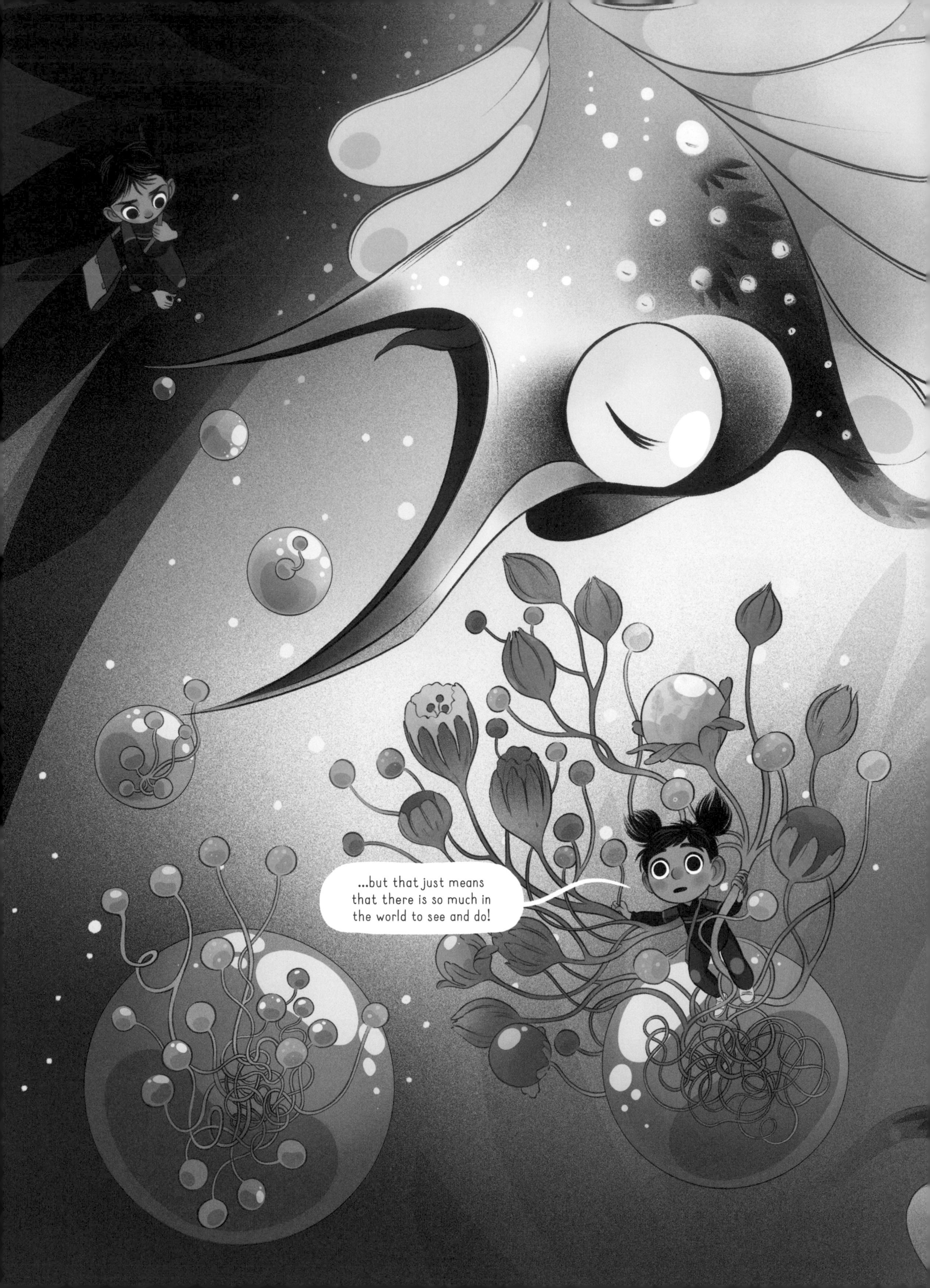
...but that just means that there is so much in the world to see and do!

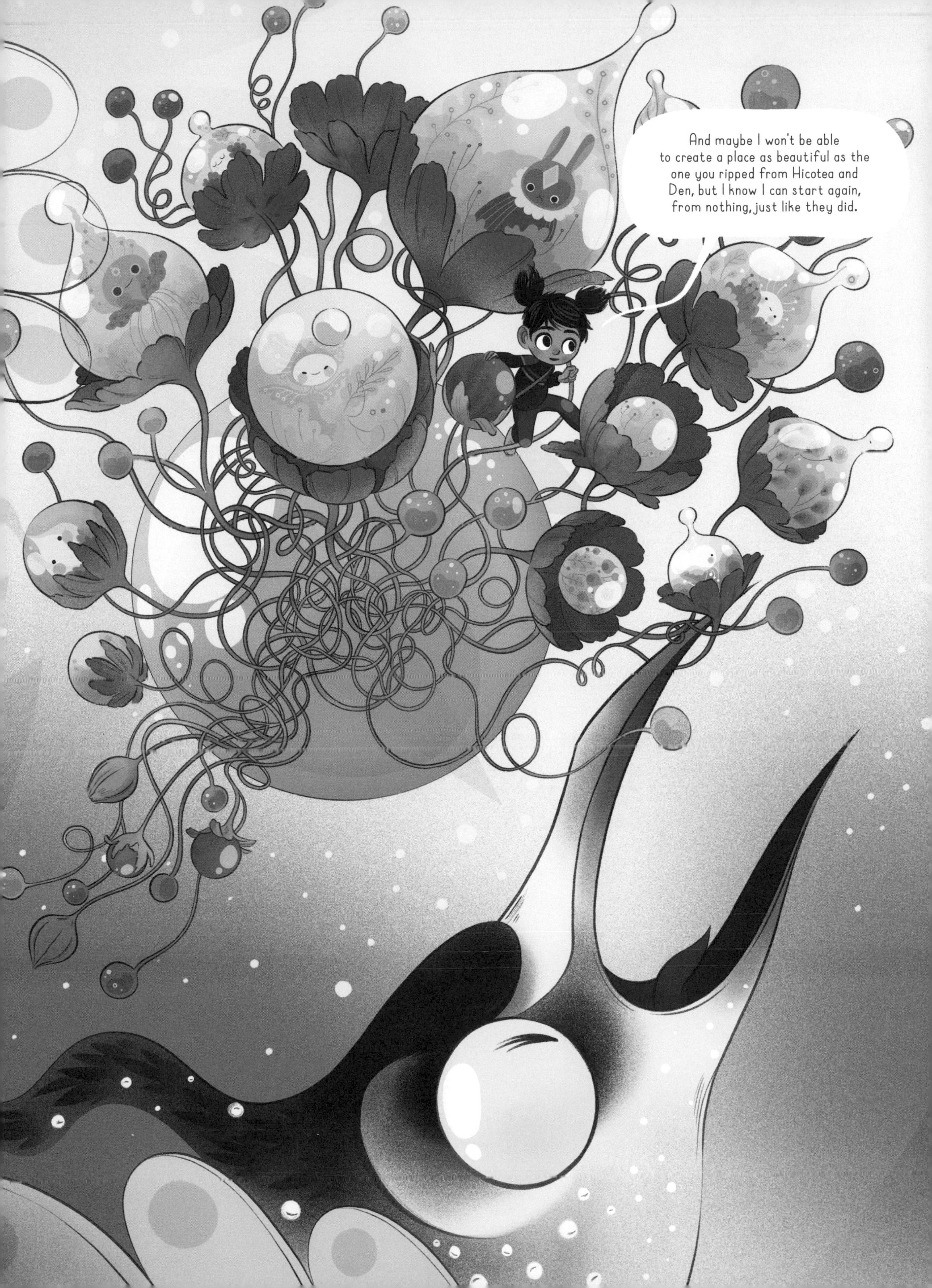
And maybe I won't be able to create a place as beautiful as the one you ripped from Hicotea and Den, but I know I can start again, from nothing, just like they did.

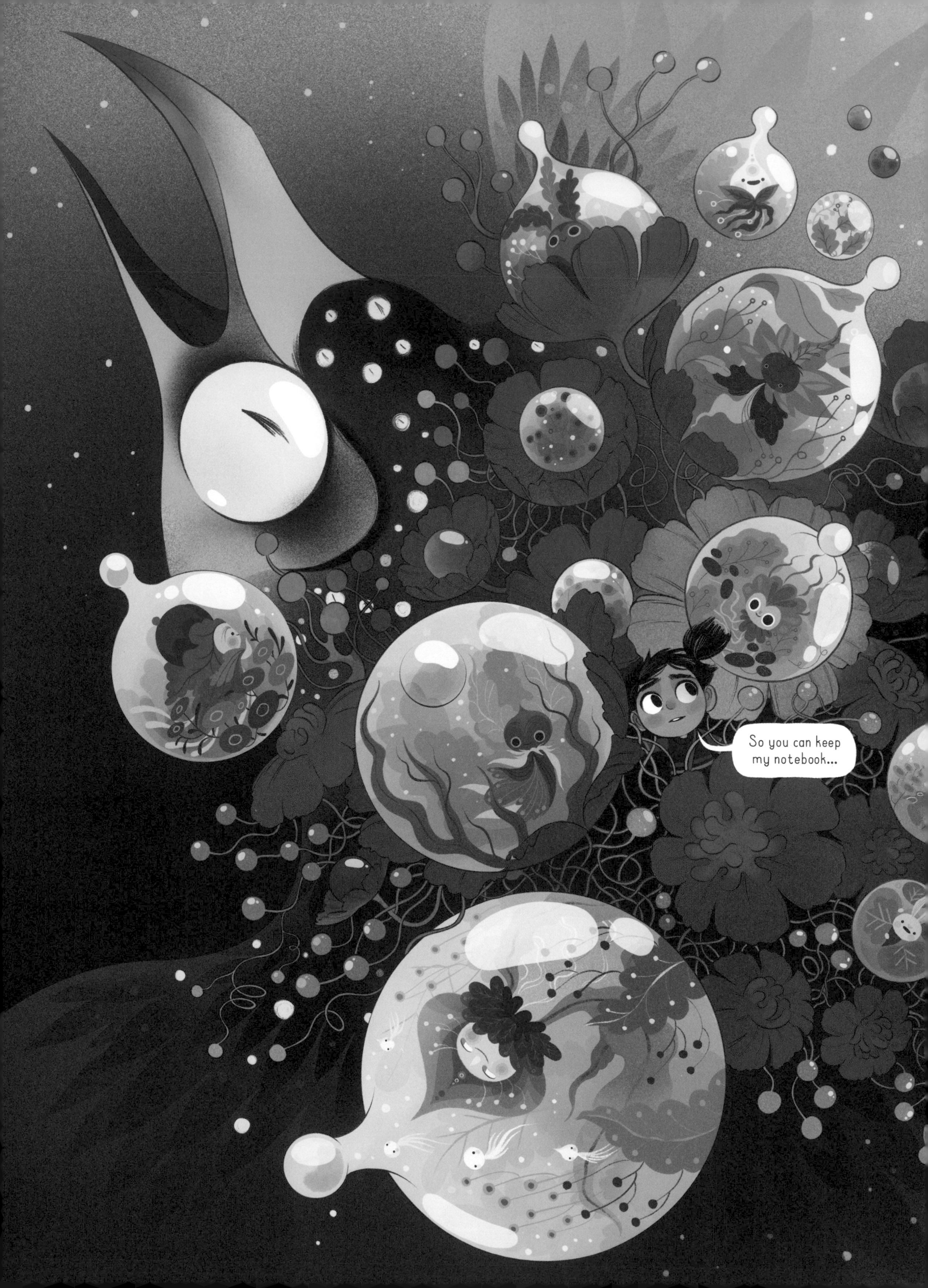
So you can keep my notebook...

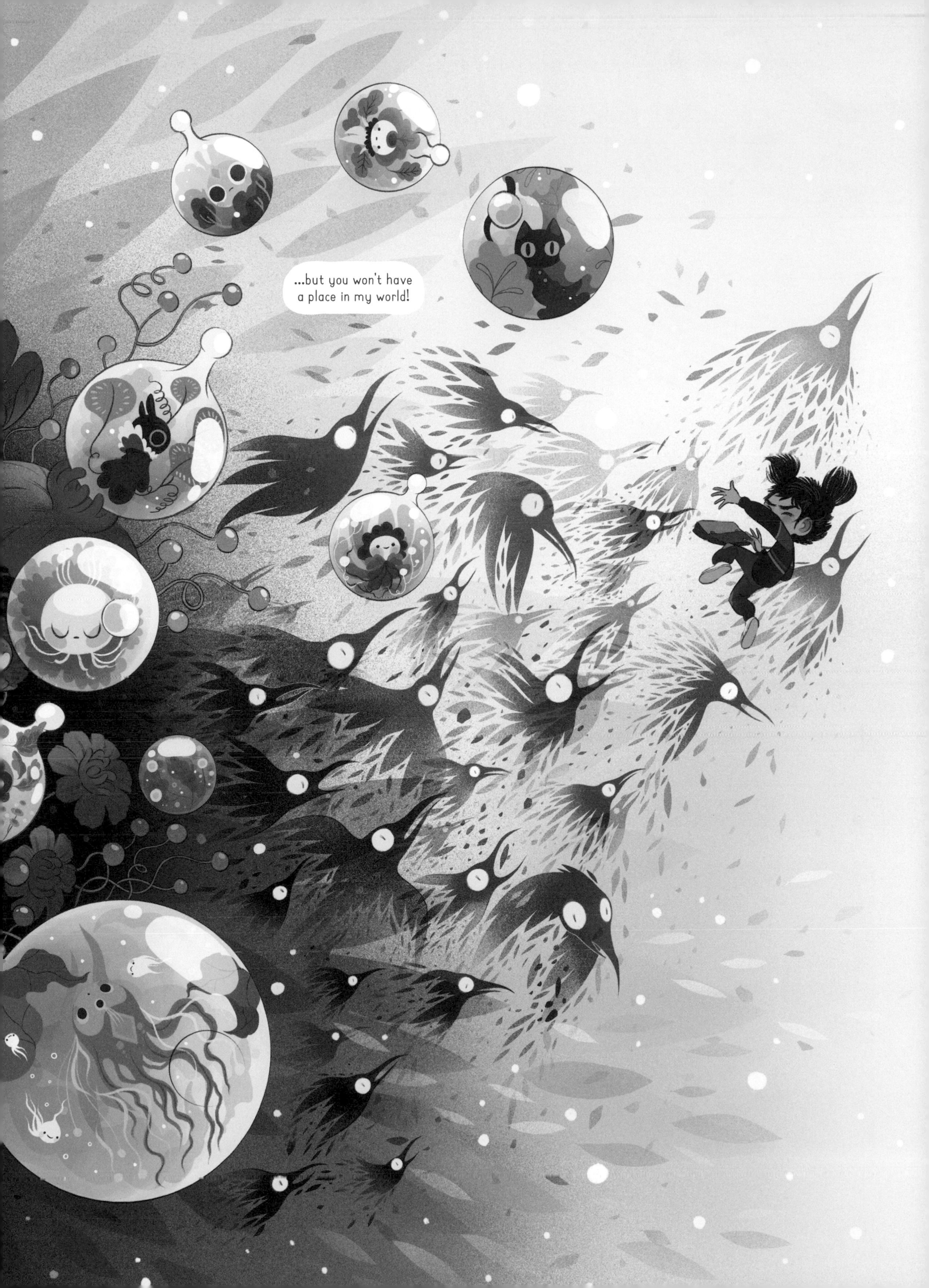
...but you won't have
a place in my world!

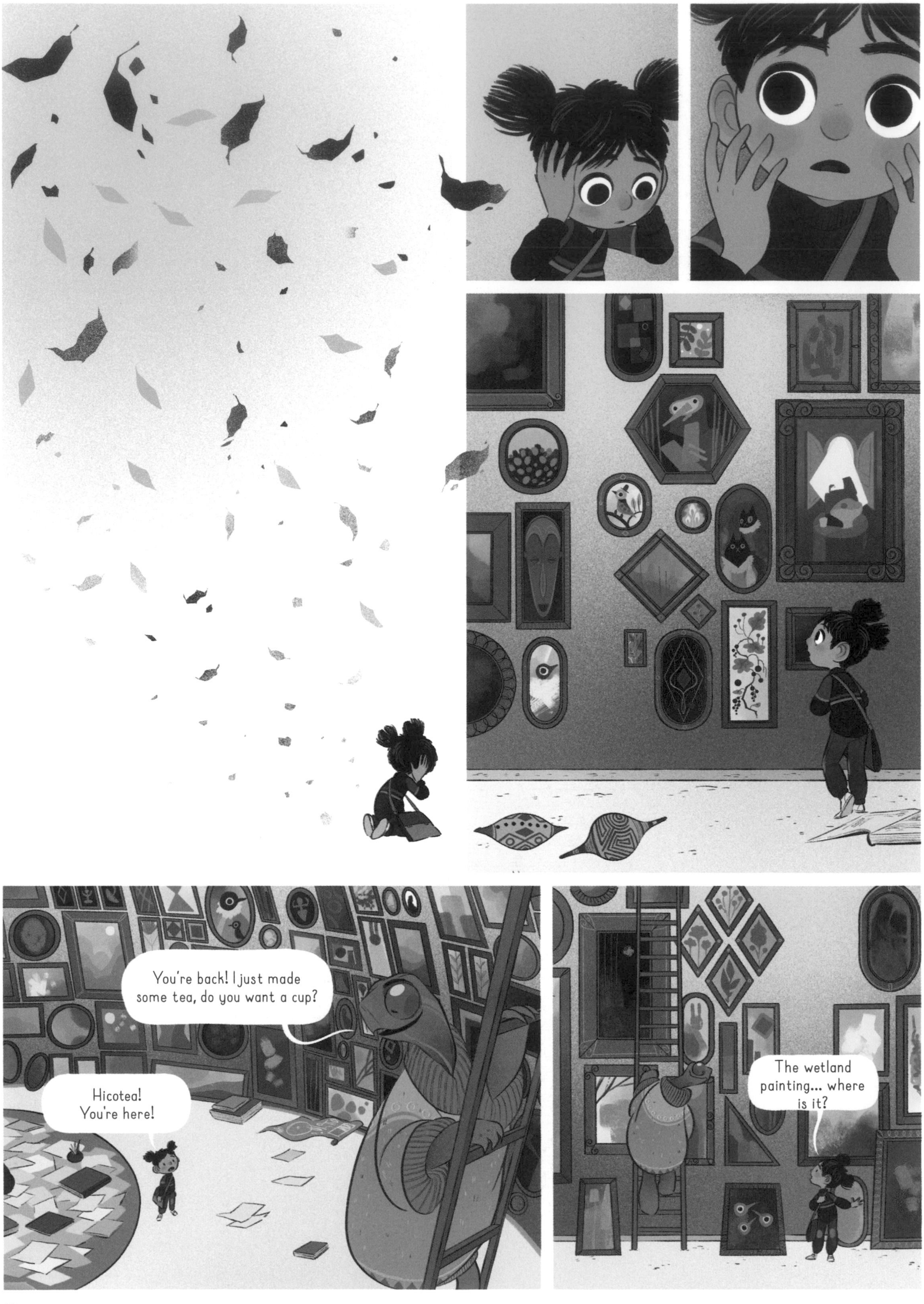
Hicotea!
You're here!
You're back! I just made
some tea, do you want a cup?
The wetland
painting... where
is it?

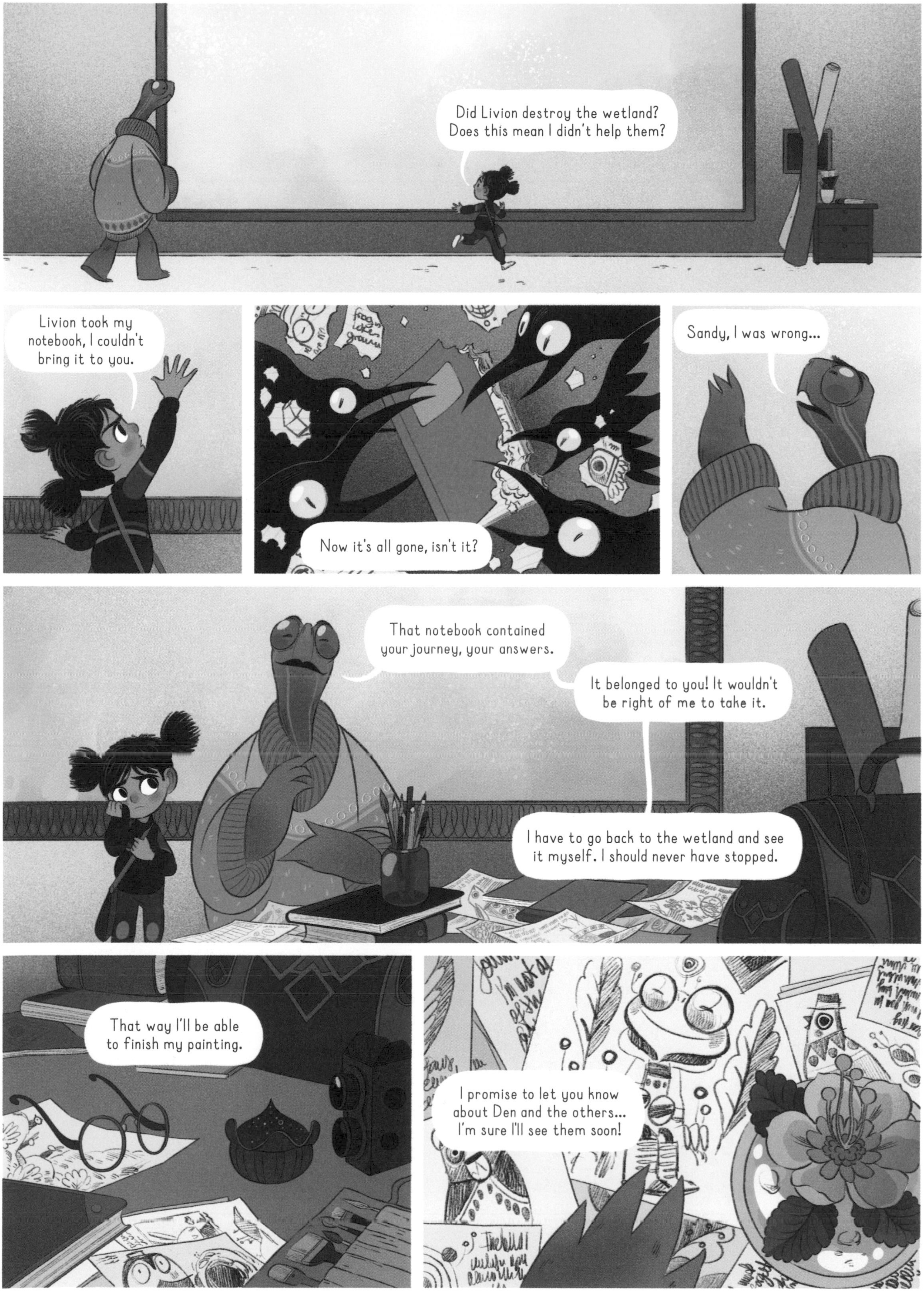
Did Livion destroy the wetland? Does this mean I didn't help them?
Livion took my notebook, I couldn't bring it to you.
Now it's all gone, isn't it?
Sandy, I was wrong...
That notebook contained your journey, your answers.
It belonged to you! It wouldn't be right of me to take it.
I have to go back to the wetland and see it myself. I should never have stopped.
That way I'll be able to finish my painting.
I promise to let you know about Den and the others... I'm sure I'll see them soon!

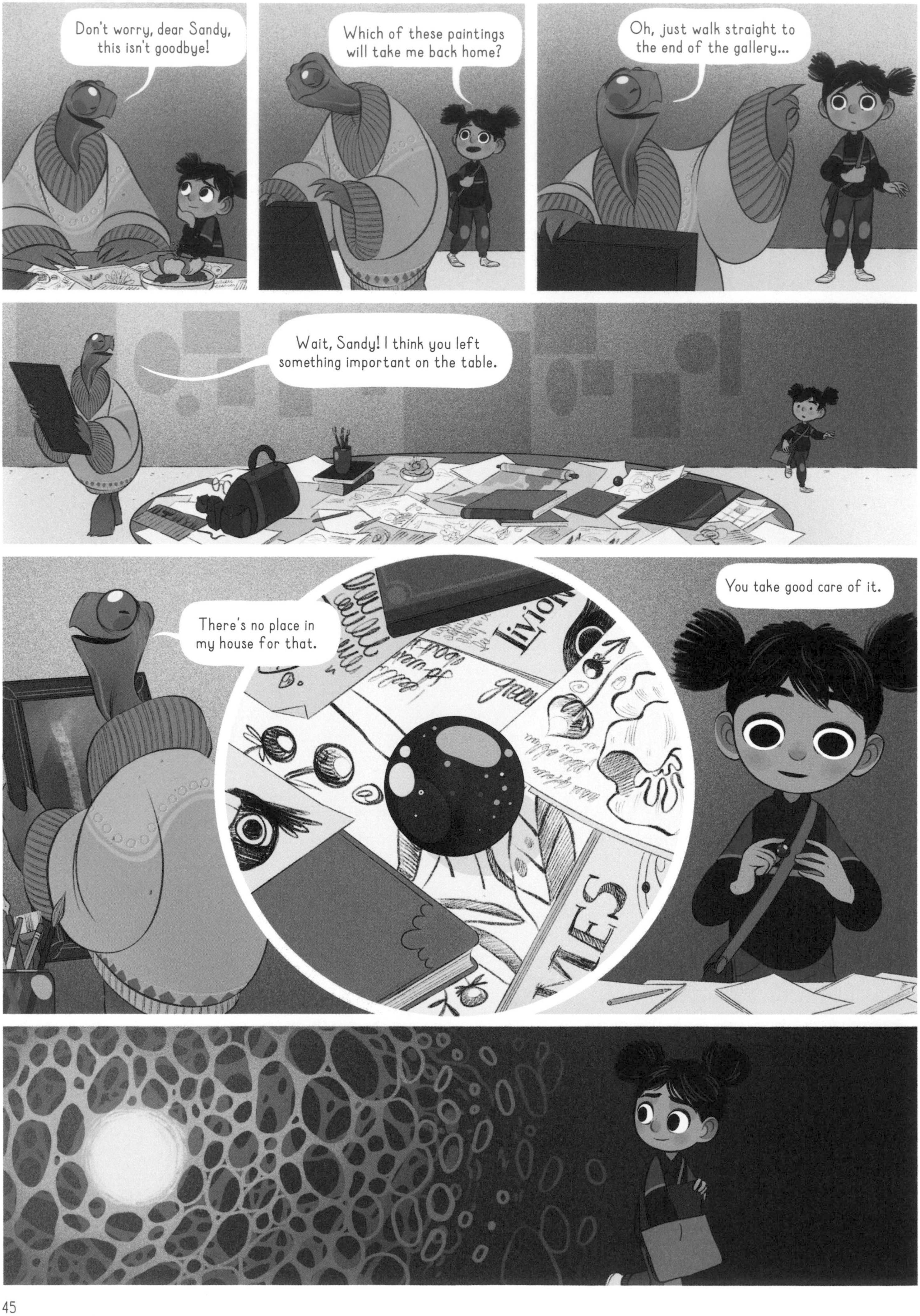
Don't worry, dear Sandy, this isn't goodbye!
Which of these paintings will take me back home?
Oh, just walk straight to the end of the gallery...
Wait, Sandy! I think you left something important on the table.
There's no place in my house for that.
You take good care of it.

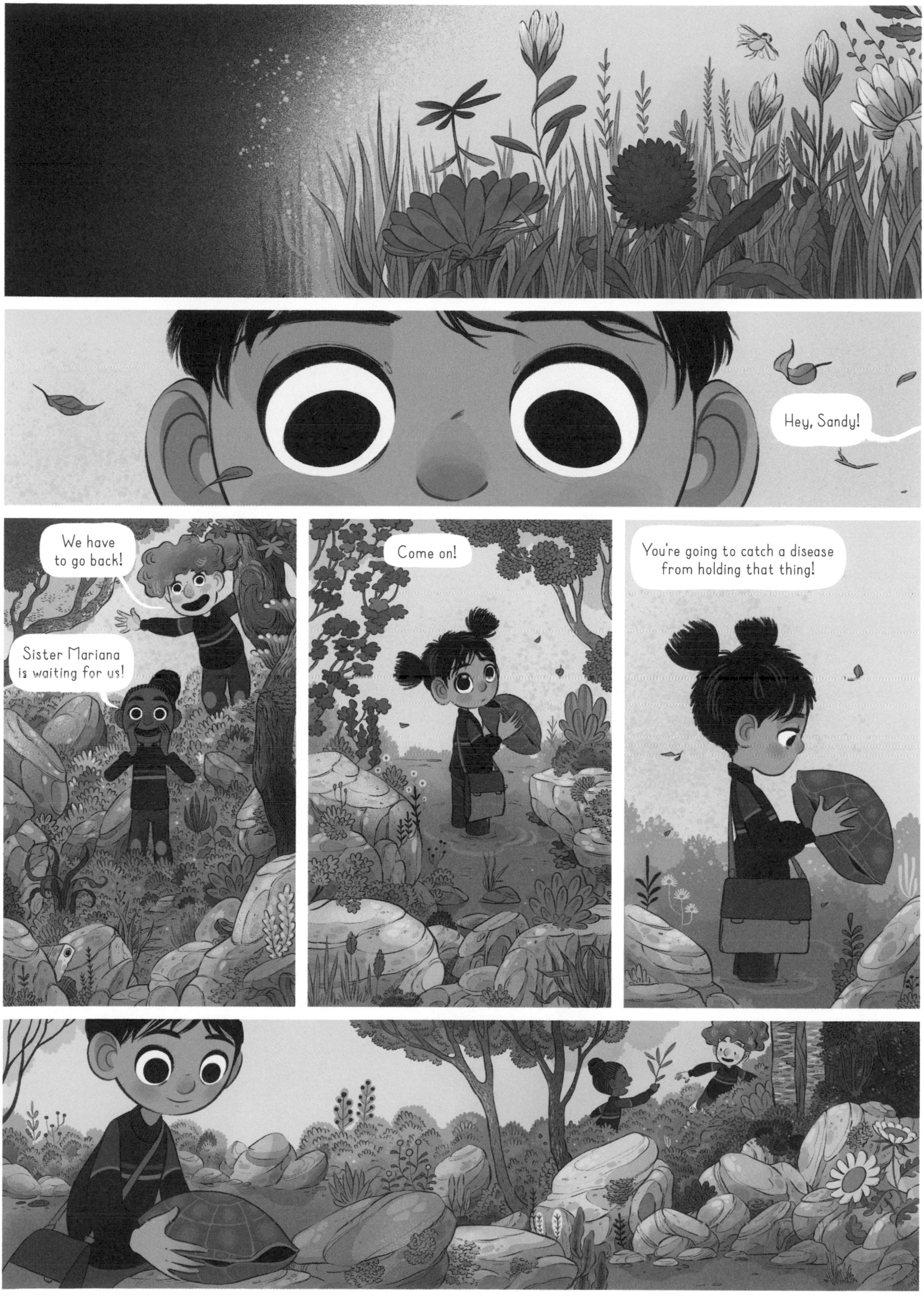
Hey, Sandy!
We have to go back!
Sister Mariana is waiting for us!
Come on!
You're going to catch a disease from holding that thing!

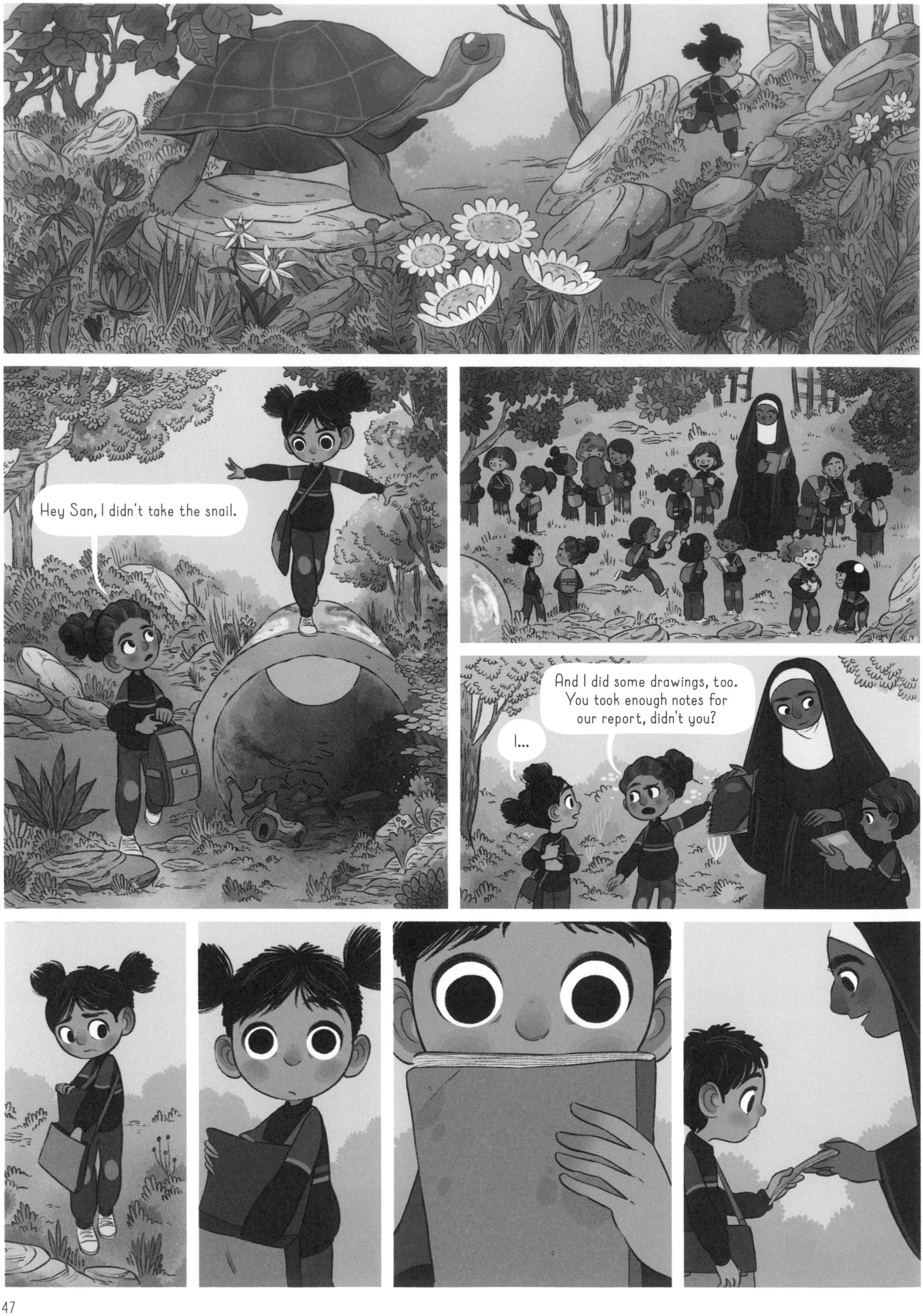
Hey San, I didn't take the snail.
And I did some drawings, too. You took enough notes for our report, didn't you?
I...

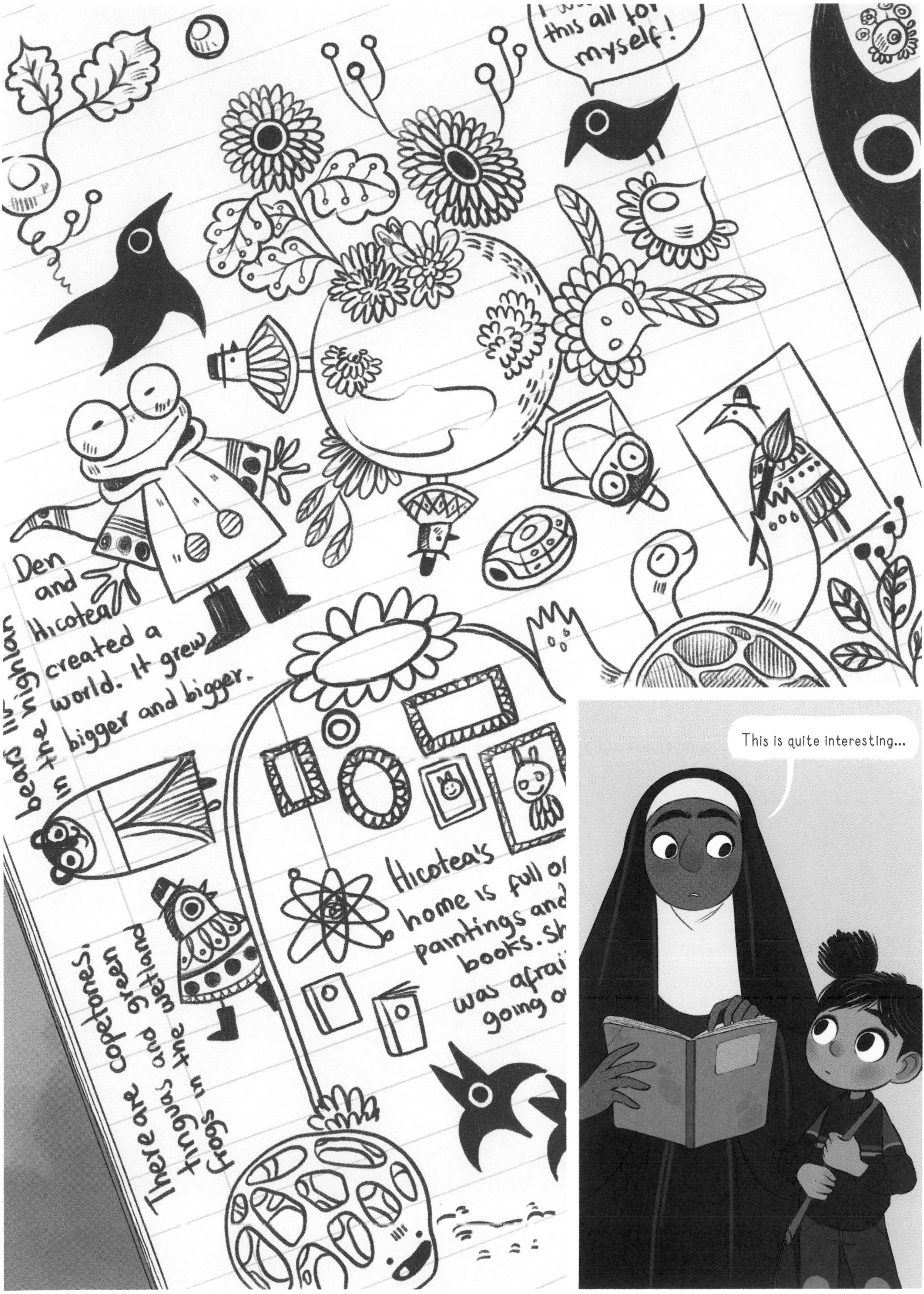

this all for myself!
Den and Hicotea created a world. It grew bigger and bigger.
bears liv
in the highlan
Hicotea's home is full o
paintings and
books. Sh
was afrai
going o
There are capetones, tinguas and green frogs in the wetland
This is quite interesting...

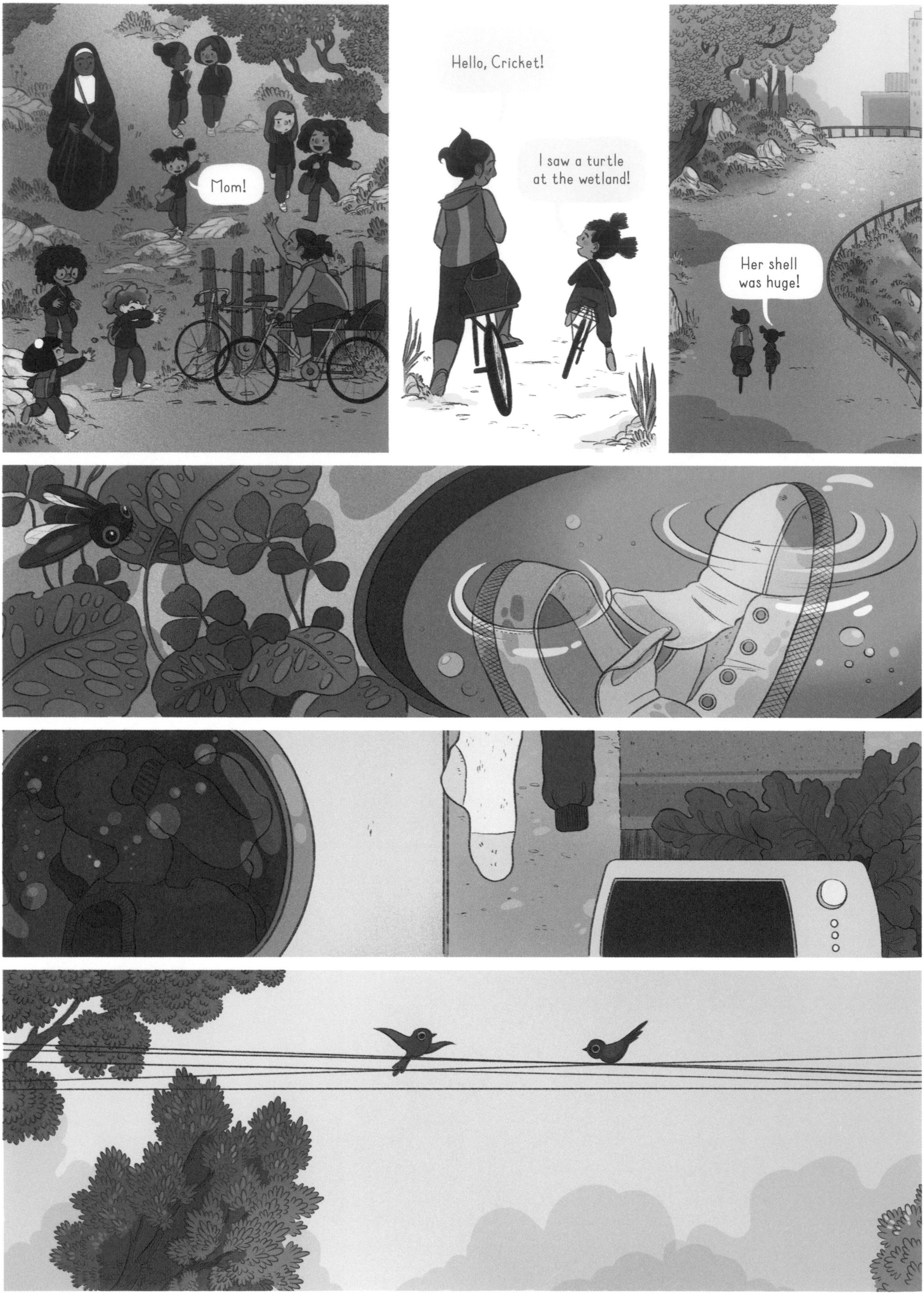
Mom!
Hello, Cricket!
I saw a turtle at the wetland!
Her shell was huge!

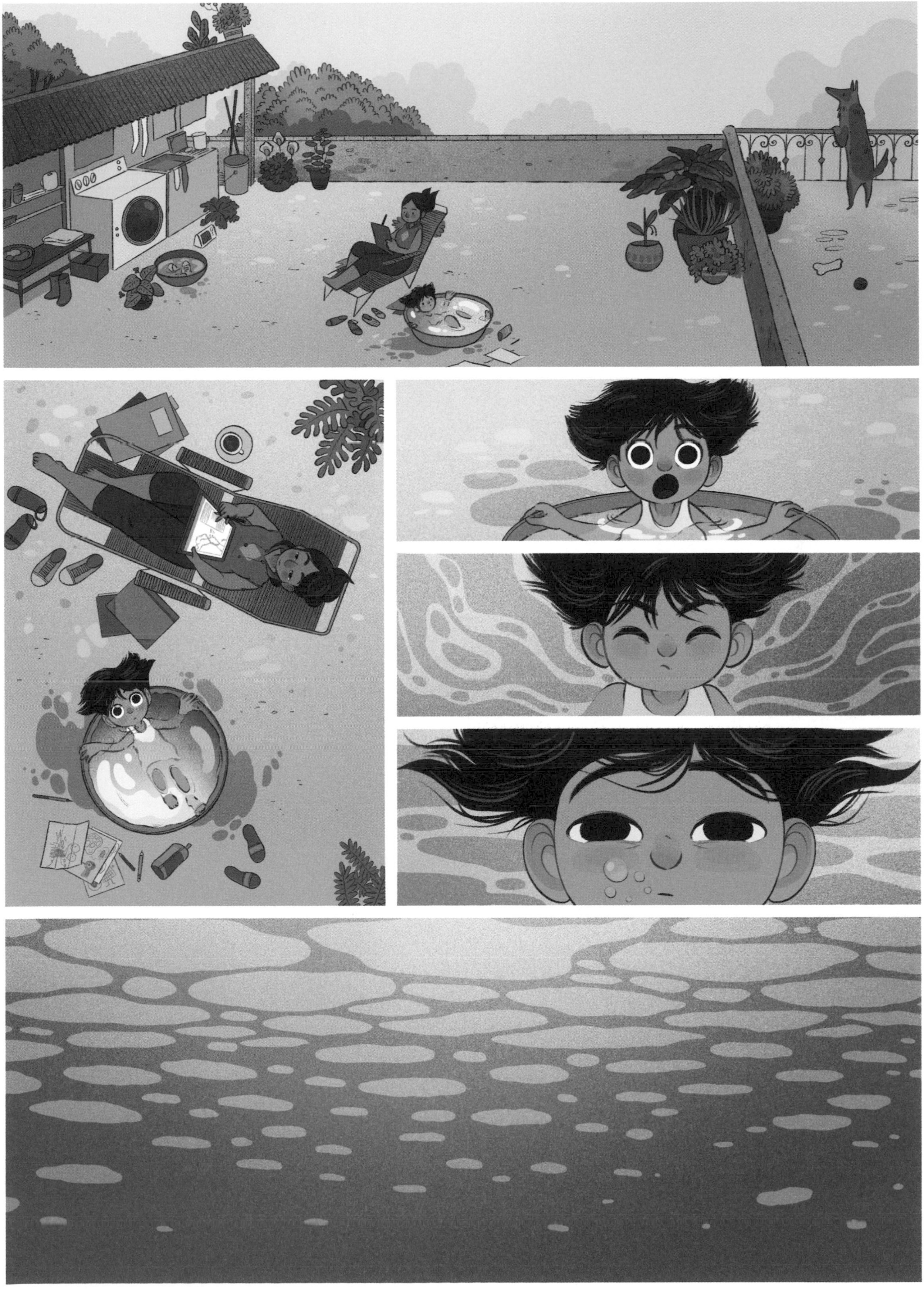

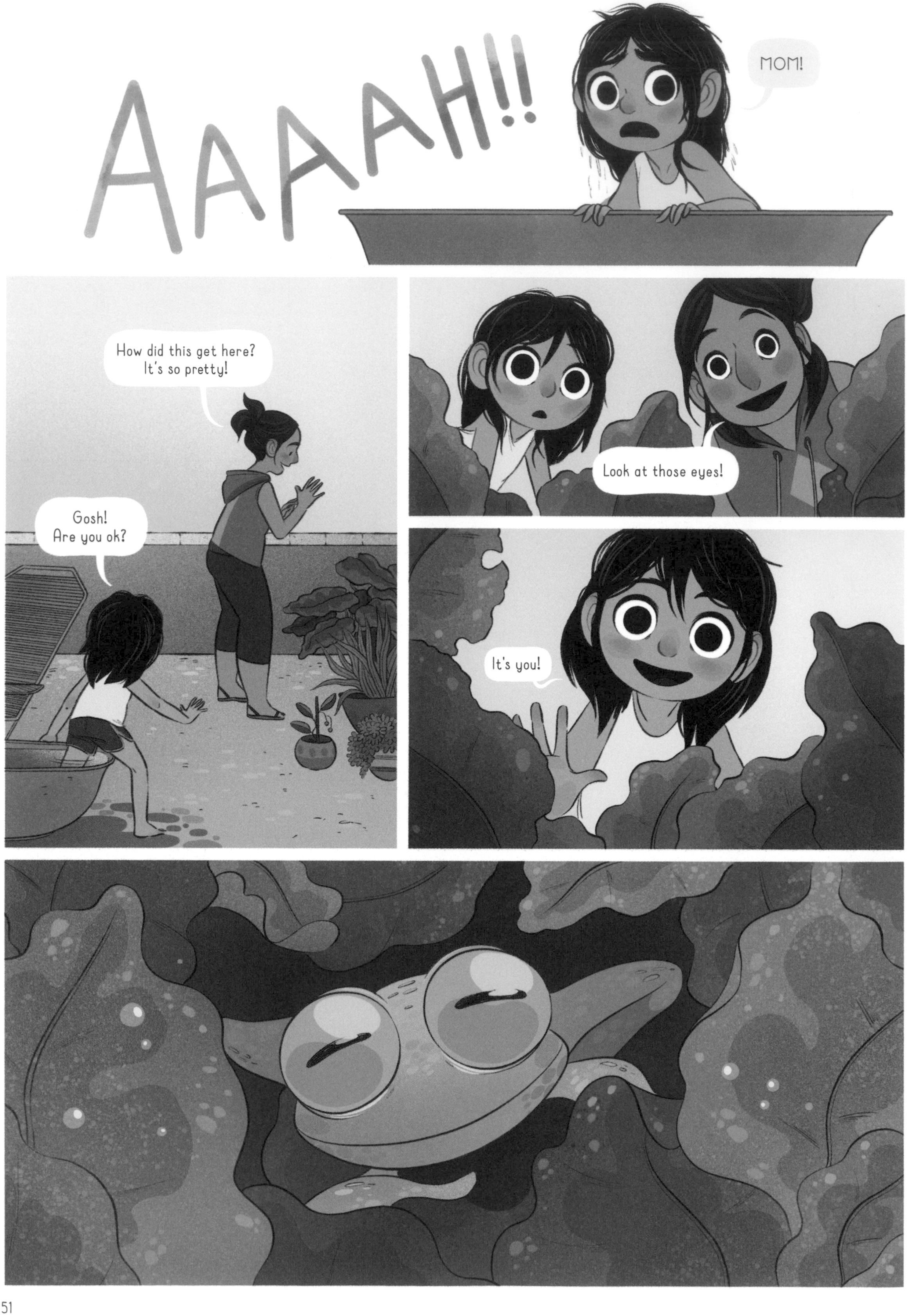
AAAAH!!
MOM!
How did this get here? It's so pretty!
Gosh! Are you ok?
Look at those eyes!
It's you!

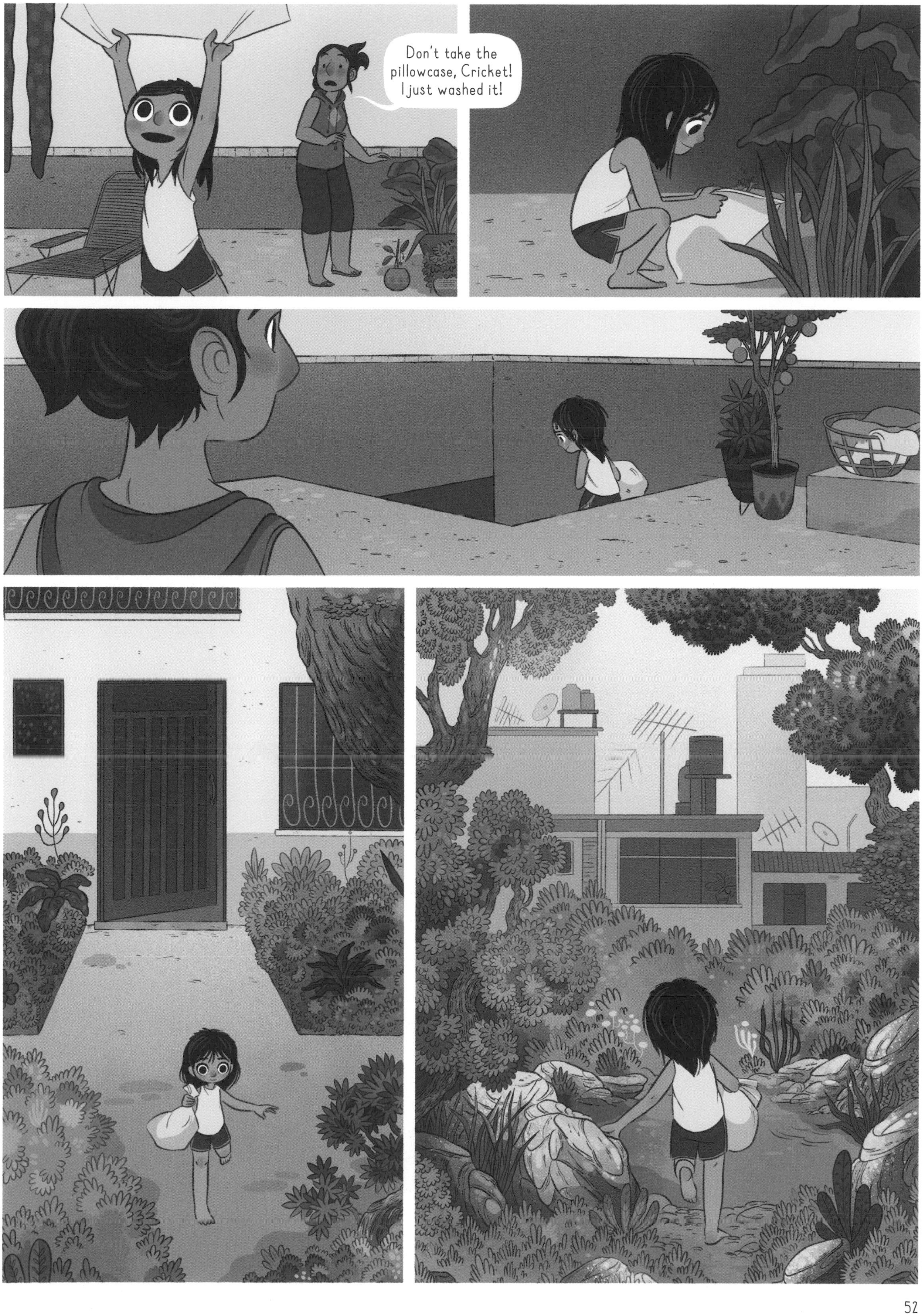
Don't take the pillowcase, Cricket! I just washed it!

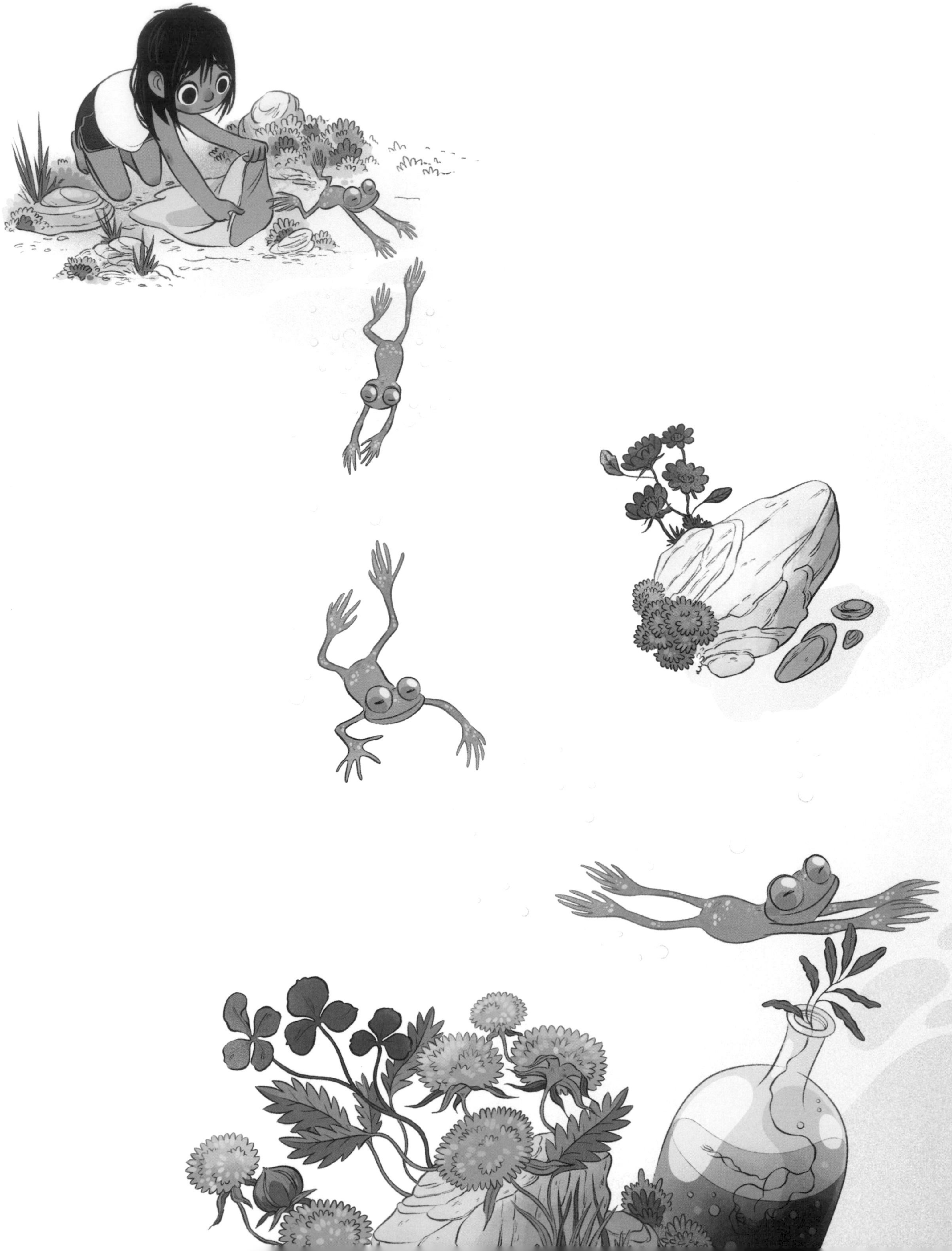

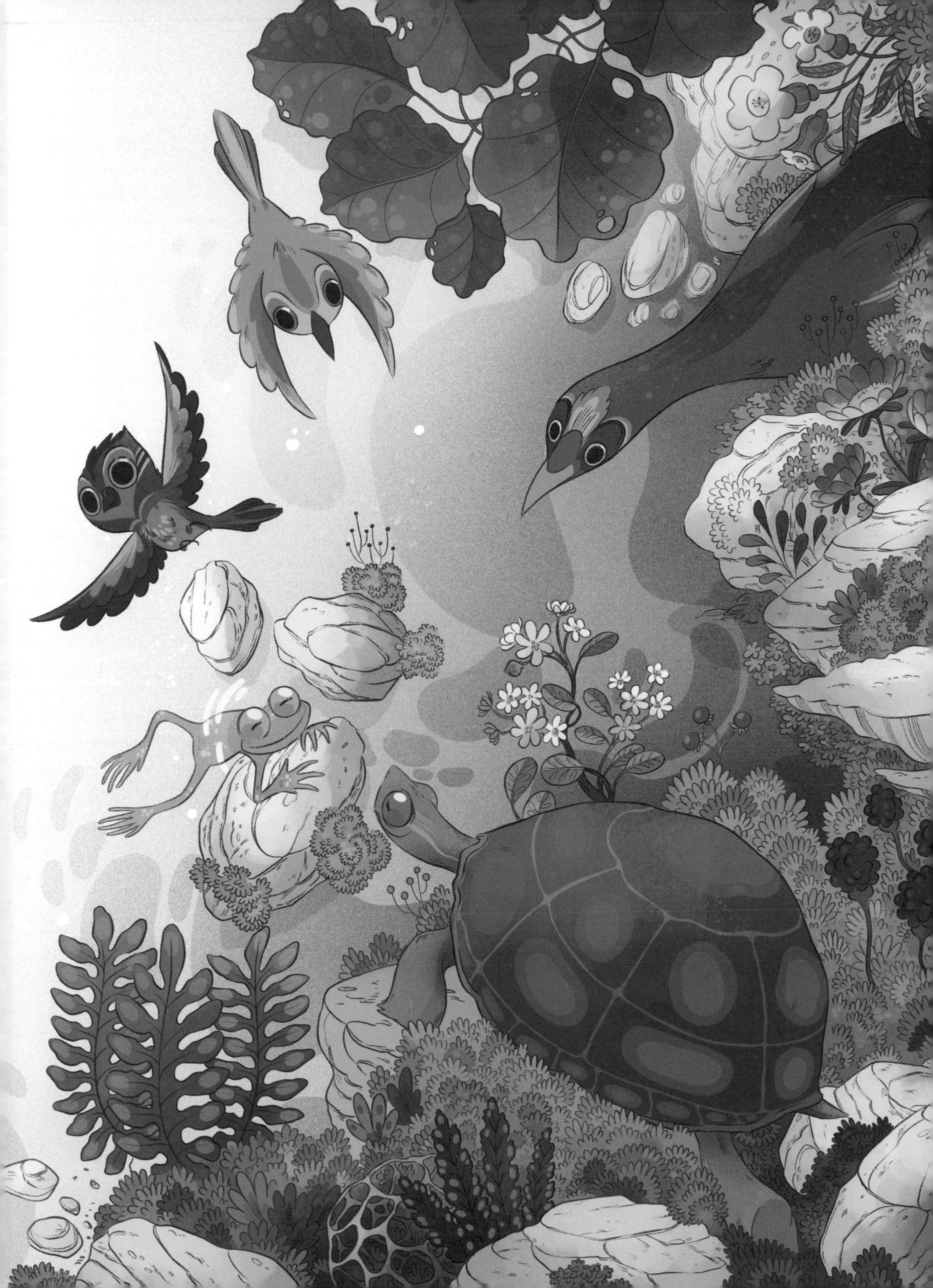

Read the first instalment of the
unforgettable series from Lorena Alvarez:

Nightlights

Hardback: 978-1-910620-13-7
Paperback: 978-1-910620-57-1

First published in 2019 by Nobrow Ltd.
27 Westgate Street, London E8 3RL.

10 9 8 7 6 5 4 3 2 1

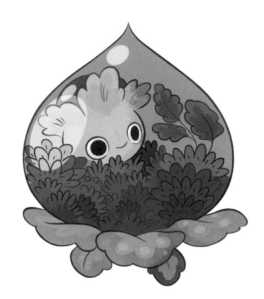

Published in the US by Nobrow (US) Inc.
Printed in Poland on FSC® certified paper.

MIX
Paper from responsible sources
FSC www.fsc.org FSC® C001693

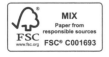

ISBN: 978-1-910620-34-2

www.nobrow.net

• Lorena Alvarez •

Born and raised in Bogotá, Colombia, Lorena's work
is influenced by the vibrancy and colour of her home town
as well as the experiences and atmosphere of the
Catholic school she attended as a child.

She studied Graphic Design and Arts at the
Universidad Nacional de Colombia, and has since
illustrated for children's books, independent publications,
advertising and fashion magazines.

Hicotea is the second instalment in the *Nightlights* series.